Romany on the Fells

Phil Shelley
with
Leonard Hollands

Illustrations

R Leonard Hollands

Lamorna Publications

Romany, as a young man, with his parents

Note that it is signed Gypsy Evens – he had not yet adopted the name Romany

Lamorna Publications
Yew Tree Studio, Marshwood, Dorset DT6 5QF
www.lamornapublications.co.uk

First published in 2011

©Phil Shelley 2011

Illustrations © R Leonard Hollands 2011

All rights reserved

ISBN: 978-0-9559832-2-1

Set in 11pt Verdana

Contents

List of Photographs

*There are two dedications: one to the
memory of Arthur Kidd, of Glassonby,
Cumbria; the second to Foxy, for inspiring
me to new life*

PS

Introduction

This is the second book I have written using the name 'Romany,' although the writing this time has been in part by Leonard Hollands. If you haven't read 'Romany in the Lanes,' I should tell you that I am not Romany himself – he died in 1943, some years before I was born. However, I have been a fan of his writing for many years, and felt it was wrong that none of his books were in new print (you could only buy them second-hand,) so, in 2007, I decided to do something positive about it, and write a new one of my own. The success of my first venture into the literary world has prompted me to write another.

Let me set the scene. Imagine, if you can, a world quite different to today. A world in which there is no television and no computer games, where the internet is not even a dream, where a motor car is so rare, that people rush from their homes to see one as it approaches, and where, in many cases, not even street lights brighten the dark nights. In this world, the radio, then known as the 'wireless,' was the more common form of home entertainment. And, it was as a result of a programme called 'Out with Romany,' that the main character of this book became the nation's favourite, with a listening audience of 13 million each week. Romany would drive out into the countryside in his horse-drawn, Gypsy caravan and take two youngsters out on nature rambles. Accompanying them were, of course, the horse, Comma, and Romany's cocker spaniel dog, called Raq. Their adventures formed the basis of the programme. In his books, however, there was a slightly different format, and a young boy appeared, instead of the two children. His name was Tim.

Now, in *my* last book, Romany met George Swalwell, the son of a farmer. George is a real person, still living in North Yorkshire. In his youth he knew Romany, who actually modelled 'Tim' on him, and used *their* real-life adventures to inspire his writing.

In 'Romany on the Fells,' our hero travels to a farm run by the Potter family. Like George, they were real people too, as was yet another farm boy, Arthur Kidd. Indeed, it was only at Easter time, in 2007, that Arthur's long life came to an end. I am proud to say that he was a friend of mine, and Leonard's, who had a fund of stories to tell about the times he spent on the farm in the company of Romany.

This book is, in part, my little tribute to a wonderful, caring man, who always displayed a sharp sense of fun. Arthur, we miss you, and the world is a poorer place for your passing...

Phil Shelley, near Liverpool, September 2011

Arthur Kidd 1918 – 2007

Editorial Note

All the characters mentioned in this book once Romany has arrived in Cumbria, or Cumberland as it would have been in Romany's day, are *real* people. However, to maximise the opportunities in the weaving of this tale, a certain amount of licence has been allowed. For example, the age difference between Arthur Kidd and Thomas Pattinson has been 'adjusted' to allow them to go 'out with Romany' together.

In fact Arthur Kidd went to Maughanby School in Glassonby – it has since closed – and later to Penrith Grammar School, but in the book he attends Kirkoswald School. This alteration to historic fact has been made so as to build on the links that have been forged over the past few years between The Romany Society and Kirkoswald School. It is hoped that this book will further enthuse the pupils of the school to pursue their interest in Romany and wildlife generally.

Romani words are given in italics. There is a Glossary at the back of the book.

Acknowledgements

The authors gratefully acknowledge the assistance given by various people in the form of local knowledge, and photographs. We would especially thank:

David and Jacquie Kidd for family photographs and details of Arthur's life.

Thomas Pattinson, seventy years a Methodist preacher, for information about his family when at Gamblesby during Romany's lifetime, and for details of Romany himself. Also for allowing us to reproduce the drawing of St John's Church, Gamblesby by Rev Sinclair Walker.

Des Potter, Edith Stockdale and David and Anne Raine for general background information about the area and Old Parks in particular.

Peter Wilson for assistance with the flora and fauna of Cumbria.

Kirkoswald School for providing a copy of Bill Roberts' book, *The History of Kirkoswald School 1856-2006*

The unknown photographer of our Frontispiece. Given the age of the photograph we assume that we have not infringed copyright by reproducing it. If any infringement has taken place the authors and publishers apologise.

Chapter 1

A difficult start

It felt good to be back on the road. Although I had enjoyed my time at Cragg Farm, in North Yorkshire, something in my Gypsy blood was urging me to move on. Only this morning I had brought Comma, my horse, to my caravan (which I call the *vardo* – its Gypsy name), harnessed her to the shafts and away we went.

All through the summer, I, and George Swalwell, my young friend from the farm, had shared many adventures, but as the weather slowly began to change and the final harvests were being gathered I recognised that if I wanted to be in Cumberland before winter, it was time to make a move. After all, we had in excess of a hundred miles to travel, with some beautiful countryside to pass through. I estimated that, at fifteen miles a day, allowing time for rests, it might take up to ten days to complete the trip.

As my old *vardo* swayed gently from side-to-side, the sweet and pleasant smell of burning stubble filled the air as I passed farm after farm where teams of workers had tried very hard to ensure that the crop was gathered in before the weather broke. I slipped into a daydream, and my mind wandered at random, back and forth in time: backwards to my adventures with George and forwards to unknown, but eagerly anticipated exploits, with an equally young Arthur Kidd. He, like George, was the son of a farmer, however, that is where the similarity ended. Unlike George, he did not live on the farm to which my *vardo* was pointing; his father worked at Midtown Farm in the nearby village, called Glassonby, and my objective lay perhaps a mile, or so, beyond it.

My journey was to be a long one, but one I was sure to enjoy; there would be so many new places to see, new people to meet and a wealth of birds and animals to encounter along the way, so it was very unlikely that I would become bored!

We had just crested a small hill, when my thoughts were shattered by Comma suddenly making a startled whinnying cry and bolting. The *vardo* jerked violently to the other side of the road and so extreme was the movement that poor Raq, my cocker spaniel dog, was flung from the running board, where he had been dozing. However, I had no time to spare for him, for, coming towards me at some speed, was a large farm waggon, being pulled by two heavy shire horses.

I could see the farmer tugging hard on the reins in a desperate attempt to slow down; I was trying exactly the same with Comma, with only a limited degree of success. I was gently repeating, "Whoa, Comma, lass," in the hope that I could calm her; I had no idea what might have caused my normally placid animal to take such fright.

It seemed that time moved in slow motion, although in reality only a few seconds passed. With mere inches to spare, I yelled to the oncoming farmer, "You go left!"

He heaved his waggon as I had directed, and I pulled the *vardo* to my left. There was a loud crash as there was contact between the two vehicles. Then, almost as suddenly as it happened, there was a silence, broken only by Raq whimpering from somewhere behind me.

I jumped from the running board and ran back to him. He was lying on the grass verge where he had landed and I must say he looked a sorry state. Now anyone who knows me will be aware of how important my animals are in my life; I was heartbroken to think that poor old Raq might be seriously hurt.

I touched him gently on his head and he growled, which I took to be a bad sign. A more faithful dog you couldn't wish to meet, and his aggression was totally out of character.

Breathlessly, the farmer ran to me, saying, "That was a close call. Are you and your dog alright?"

I replied, "I am, thanks, but I'm concerned about Raq, here. He was thrown from the caravan."

"It was that damned snake that did it," he responded. "It was crossing right in front of you."

I had to admit I hadn't noticed it, but clearly Comma had and it had spooked her.

"Shall I fetch the vet?" he kindly offered.

"Thank you. I think that's sensible," I said.

"I'll phone him from the farm," were his parting words, as he ran back to his waggon.

I took off my jacket and placed it lightly over the dog. He looked up at me with those saucer-sized eyes, of his and my heart melted. What can be worse than a helpless animal in pain? I said, "Don't worry, old man, help will soon be here," to which his stubby tail responded with a feeble wag; not at all the normal dynamo-like effort to which I had become so used to seeing.

An age seemed to pass as we waited for the arrival of the vet. I had no idea how far away he might be. Would Raq be able to withstand the wait?

Then, in the distance, I heard the sound of a motor engine. I hoped against hope that it would be the vet. The sound grew louder and then, from over the same hill that we had ourselves travelled, came a small car. It came to a halt behind the *vardo*, and out jumped a red-faced man, carrying a leather medical bag.

"I'm Johnson, the vet, and you must be Romany," he said.

I didn't think to question how he might know my name; my only concern was for Raq. I briefly explained what had happened as he knelt beside the now silent dog.

"It will be best to start with an anaesthetic," he said. "He's been in a lot of pain, and it will only distress him more as I examine him."

He quickly administered the needle and within seconds Raq visibly relaxed.

The vet ran his hands over him, muttering to himself all the time. Once, I thought I detected the word 'good,' but I couldn't be sure.

At last, he stood up and announced, "I don't think there's anything serious, here, Romany. He's lucky he landed on the grass and not on the road. I would just like to take him back to the surgery for an x-ray, to be safe. I can take him and bring him back, if that's OK with you?"

I simply nodded my approval to him, too worried to speak. Apart from my hospitalisation in Whitby, which I mentioned at the end of my last book, Raq and I had not been parted since I bought him from the Grey Stoke Kennels in Halifax, when he was a young pup. I managed to say that I would park the *vardo* on the roadside, so that he would know where to find me.

We gingerly lifted the little animal on to the back seat of the car. Through the window, I took a long look at him as the kindly vet climbed into the driver's seat, closed the door, and started the engine. He slowly and deliberately turned his car around. It disappeared over the brow of the hill and I was left alone with my thoughts. I turned to the *vardo*, and, with Comma's help, manoeuvred it into a place of safety on the wide grass verge. I secured the wheels with a few large stones wedged beneath them and released the horse from the shafts. She set-to munching the grass, but I didn't want her to have too much and quickly fitted her nosebag, filled with oats, which are much better for her health. The air was filled with the sound of her contented munching.

My thoughts turned to my own food, but I had little appetite, too worried about how Raq might be faring at the vet's surgery.

Then I remembered the crashing sound as the *vardo* had struck the waggon. Apprehensively, I took a look at the right-hand side of the caravan. Luckily, although the paintwork was badly scraped, there was no serious damage. I made a note that I would put things right when we were settled on the farm.

I turned-in for the night, but slept fitfully, with dreams buzzing around inside my head, just like angry bees. Needless to say, my dreams were nightmares, filled with an injured Raq, accidents to the *vardo*, and huge snakes.

Chapter 2

Underway again

The following morning I was up and about at five o'clock, feeling, and, no doubt looking, the worse for wear. I washed and shaved and prepared for the day ahead. During the night the awful thought occurred to me that I hadn't asked the vet where his surgery was located; I had absolutely no idea how I could contact him. I hadn't even asked the farmer where he lived! How could I have been so stupid? I was completely in the hands of the vet and who knew when he might return; today, tomorrow, next week, next year? What would I do? Other than staying put, I couldn't think of any viable alternatives.

I tidied around the inside of the *vardo* and then the outside camp area, but, in truth, there was little to do. I had only spent one night there and had not really had time to create a mess, but at least it kept me busy while I awaited news of my faithful dog.

I had just made the decision to mop-out the already spotless *vardo*, when the now familiar sound of an approaching car made me rush towards the door. Sure enough, the vet was pulling alongside.

Anxiously, I peered into the vehicle, and there was Raq, barking and wagging his tail!

The vet's first words were, "He's about as tough as old boots, Romany!"

He went on to explain that he had no broken bones and appeared only to have been stunned by the fall. I had to make sure he didn't take too much exercise over the next few days - no leaping over walls, for instance - and things should be back to normal. The relief I felt on hearing this news was extreme, which must have been obvious to the vet, as he said, "We do get attached to our pets, don't we?"

I gently lifted Raq from the back seat of the car, where I had placed him only the evening before, and carried him to the *vardo*, where I laid him on his bed under the bench seat. I turned to the vet, who had followed me up the steps, saying, "How can I ever thank you, Mr Johnson? He looked so poorly last night that I honestly thought the worst, and had prepared myself for bad news this morning."

"I'm only too glad to be able to help you both, Romany. It's not often a famous dog comes to my surgery!" the vet replied.

"You called me Romany yesterday, but in my anxiety I never thought to ask how you knew me," I responded.

"Simple, really," he said. I'd heard you were in these parts. My family are real fans of your programme on the wireless, and of your books, too, and I'd seen your picture in some of them. Then I made a simple deduction: a man in a Gypsy caravan – sorry, I mean *vardo*, with a cocker spaniel called Raq. Who else might it be, but Romany?"

"You would put Sherlock Holmes to shame, Mr Johnson," I laughed. "Now to the serious business; what do I owe you for his treatment?"

"I tell you what I'd really like, Romany," he said.

"Name your price."

"I've brought two of your books from home; would you be kind enough to autograph them for my children?"

"Well, Mr Johnson, that's an absurdly small price to pay for Raq's health, but I'd be delighted."

Usually, I sign my books, just 'Romany,' but this time I made a small pen sketch in each of them, with my name beneath. One was a skylark, singing, the other a heron waiting in the reeds to catch a fish.

"I hope your children will be happy with these," I said. "It seems a poor return for your help."

"That is just wonderful," the vet answered. "My family will treasure them," he assured me. "You get on your way, Romany. I'm sure you've got places to be."

"I was heading for a farm in Cumberland," I told him, "but this incident brought a temporary halt to that."

"This isn't an unusual place to see adders," he said. "There are quite a number of them living on the heathland to the north of the road. I've seen two, or three in my time, although they're quite secretive."

I told him that I, too, had seen adders before, once even witnessing a hedgehog in a fight with one.

He descended the steps and returned to his car. I thanked him again and waved him off.

I called Comma and harnessed her into the *vardo* shafts, checked that everything moveable was stowed away, climbed onto the running board and we were back on the road.

Because of Raq's need for rest, I pulled Comma back into a gentler pace than she would normally prefer, which seemed the right thing to do at this stage in the dog's recovery process. Moving so slowly, I might need to allow for another three days on top of the ten I had first bargained for. No matter; I had not told the Potter family, who owned the farm in Cumberland, when to expect me. They knew my Gypsy habits; arrive when you like, go to bed when you like, move on whenever the mood takes you. They would have no concerns and would expect me only when they saw the *vardo* travelling down the lane that led into their farmyard.

For several hours we trotted pleasantly down the lanes and byways, seeing very little traffic, with just the occasional horse-drawn vehicle approaching. So far, Raq had made no move to join me, preferring to rest on his bed. However, I eventually became aware of a faint whimpering sound coming from inside the *vardo*, so I pulled Comma to the side of road and stopped. Going back into the darker interior, I could see Raq had got to his feet, but he looked distinctly uncomfortable. Reasoning that he wanted to go outside to stretch his legs, I fitted the steps to the front of the caravan and then went back to him, and bent down, saying, "Come along, old man; let's get you outside." Very carefully, I lifted him and carried him down to the grass verge, where I placed him on the ground. He sniffed the air and I left him to wander around for a couple of minutes.

He walked about a little, but just wasn't the old Raq. Gone was his habit of darting backwards and forwards with his nose pressed to the ground; a nose that told him of every wild creature that had passed that way during the last few days. It made me sad to see him like that, a dog that only two days before had been so full of life, reduced to a shuffling gait.

I walked over to him and as he sensed me near, his tail began to wag just like a fan!

"That's better, Raq," I told him. "I can see this might be a long job, but I've got all the time in the world." Although he probably had no idea what I meant, his tail vibrated even more.

I put my arms beneath him and took him back on board the *vardo*. I settled him back on his bed, where he simply curled up, putting his nose against his tail.

Going back to the running board, I sat down, took up the reins, and gently urged Comma on.

A few hours passed and I judged by the position of the sun, and a growing feeling of emptiness in my stomach, that it was around time for lunch. Because I had hardly eaten anything since Raq's accident, I was feeling particularly hungry. Looking ahead for a suitable spot to pull the *vardo* off the road, I soon spied a place, alongside a dry stone wall, that would be just right. Comma slipped us into a perfect position, and I jumped down and made the wheels secure.

When all was safe, I lit the stove inside the living area of the caravan, in order to fry some bacon. I would normally prefer to cook outside on an open fire, in the traditional way, but I wanted to be close to the dog to ensure that he didn't try to jump down.

Soon the interior was filled with a sizzling sound, and a wonderful smell that made my mouth water. Cutting a few slices of bread, and removing the bacon from the pan, my simple lunch was ready. Although it was late in the year, the weather was still mild, so I went back to the step and sat there to eat, and was soon deep in thought.

Suddenly, from the corner of my eye, I saw a fleeting movement in the vicinity of the wall. It was gone almost before I recognised it, but I was certain it was a stoat. I stayed quiet and the only sound to be heard was Comma's deep breathing. Then there was a faint scratching sound and a stoat popped its head out from a gap between two stones, closer to me than where I had first seen it.

Catching sight of me, it made a funny 'chattering' noise, which made it appear rather angry. I found it quite comical that a tiny animal, not even the size of a rabbit, could shout in anger at a human being, many times its size, and it made me chuckle at its cheek. However, I knew that, despite its size, it would have no hesitation in killing a much larger animal for food.

The head disappeared as quickly as it had arrived, and I thought about how useful a dry stone wall must

Stoat

be to the animal kingdom. A resourceful farmer, who
built and maintained it, had carefully placed stone upon
stone, just like a jigsaw puzzle. Unlike regular brick
walls, the stones were a good, but imperfect match,
leaving many nooks and crannies, forming little tunnels
which harboured small creatures: mice, rats, birds, and,
of course, stoats. It would provide sufficient shelter to
make a snug, dry home for them, keeping out the
harshest weather. In spring and summer the wall was,
in effect, a huge nursery, housing many and varied
families, and it stretched for miles. It was a virtual
housing estate for feathered and furry residents, but
with no rent to pay! Inside, the inhabitants could move
around as much as they liked, probably only venturing
out to feed. A smile played on my lips as I imagined
shops, roads and street lights, rail stations and cafés!

"You're a bit old for thinking like that, Romany!" I
told myself, but it was fun to imagine.

I cleared away the lunch dishes and pan, had a drink
of cold milk, doused the fire, and made ready to move
off. I again allowed Raq down for a few minutes, and it
seemed to me that he was slightly better. He took
some interest in the wall, and I guessed he could smell
that the stoat had paid a visit.

"You just mind your nose, Raq," I told him. "Mr Stoat will nip it, and you'll need to see the vet again!"

He ambled back over to where I was waiting; I lifted him up and again placed him inside.

I was sure he was feeling better, because he looked more relaxed, as though, perhaps, his pain was easing.

"We'll soon be back to normal," I muttered, not wishing to disturb him.

With a gentle flick of the leather reins, we were underway.

Chapter 3

Camp for the night

After several more hours, when I judged that we might have travelled far enough for the first day following the accident, I began to seek a spot for the night. I carry very little water in the *vardo*, as the metal tank that holds it is quite small. Therefore, a stream or river nearby is always a feature of my campsites. Beside the obvious need for drinking water, I can almost always catch a fish for supper, assuming I can obtain permission, of course. Most rivers are owned by someone and it wouldn't do for me to be accused of poaching!

I pulled a map from a drawer behind me and found roughly where we were. There it was! Another mile, or so, and a small river came quite close to the road I was travelling. Perfect! All we needed was somewhere safe to locate the *vardo*, and a field in which to turn-out Comma.

Ahead I could see a slight bend in the road, which seemed to match the spot on the map, so I slowed the horse to a walking pace. Standing up, but still keeping hold of the reins, I could see over the wall, and sure enough I could see the river. Even better, I saw a gate, wide enough through which to drive the *vardo*.

I stopped Comma, climbed down, and threw the gate back. Then I led her through, holding the reins just underneath her chin.

It looked almost ideal; flat, solid ground (I didn't want the wheels to settle in soft earth), water nearby, a field for the horse. Now all I had to do was seek the blessing of the owner.

The map indicated a farmhouse, probably no further than half-a-mile away, so I checked that Raq was alright, locked the *vardo* door, and set-off at a brisk pace down the lane.

It felt good to be travelling under my own steam. It is nice to ride on the *vardo*, but walking in the countryside is a real pleasure, too; you are that much closer to nature.

Within ten minutes I reached the farm, setting the dogs barking as I entered the gate. A lady emerged from the front door and she smiled as I crossed the yard towards her.

She took me by complete surprise when she said, "Welcome, Mr Romany!"

"How on earth do you know who I am?" I enquired.

"Mr Johnson, the vet, telephoned to say that he thought you would be here," she explained. "He estimated how far you might travel, and he knew you'd need water, and we are the closest farm to the river. You're welcome to stay in our fields for just as long as you want."

"That man amazes me," was all I could say.

However, I didn't forget my manners, thanking the lady for her kindness. She promised that later that evening, her husband would drop some milk, eggs and bread at the *vardo*.

I left the farm and retraced my steps. Rounding the bend in the lane I stopped and gazed on a picture of perfection. There, in a lush, green field was my lovely *vardo*, with Comma grazing beside it, and a chuckling river below. There are many stunning and beautiful sights in this world, but right now nothing seemed able to equal this view. I sighed, contentedly. Give me the open road and you can keep the Seven Wonders of the World!

I leaned against the old wall, taking in the peaceful scene. For many hundreds of years my ancestors had surveyed just such a view. The smoke from their cooking fires had drifted lazily in the still autumn air, giving a homely touch to their camp. Wherever their vardos had rested for the night, babies had been born, old people had died, arguments had taken place, deals had been struck, and here I was, following my heritage. I counted myself a lucky man indeed.

I came out of my daydream and strolled down the lane, entered the field and climbed the steps to my old *vardo*.

I was greeted by a lively Raq, which made my heart feel glad. He was very obviously on the way to making a full recovery and would soon be chasing rabbits and hares; always unsuccessfully, so far, but I knew that wouldn't dampen his enthusiasm!

Later on, exactly as promised, the farmer appeared, bringing the provisions I'd asked for. We chatted for a while; he told me all that was happening on the farm, and I answered his questions about life on the road and my radio broadcasts (did I mention that I had a weekly radio programme called 'Out with Romany?') He had even brought a copy of one of my books, which I gladly autographed for him.

In answer to my enquiry about ownership of the river and possible fishing, he declared himself to be its title-holder, and that I could fish as much as I wished.

He left me with a cheery, "Night, then, Romany," and made his way to the gate and then on down the lane, where, for a good distance, I could see his hat bobbing above the wall, before finally disappearing from view.

I turned in for the night and soon fell into a deep and dreamless sleep.

The following morning I awoke early, as I usually do, and made my way down to the river, with a much brighter Raq following at my heel.

I cast my line and it wasn't too long before a couple of brown trout, which I intended to fry for breakfast, were safe within my fishing bag.

I was packing away my rod, when I spotted a movement, not by the river itself, but above a pool, some yards away.

"Looks like a very small bird," I thought. Could it be a wren, one of our smallest birds? But surely not flying up and down over water?

I withdrew my binoculars from my bag and quickly focussed on the 'bird.' To my surprise, I discovered that it was actually an insect. In fact, it was a type of dragonfly, probably about two inches long, with four wings that beat very quickly. Now I'm no dragonfly expert, preferring birds to insects, so I couldn't immediately identify the species. As I always do when I see something I don't recognise I began to mutter to myself precisely what I could see.

"Almost brown all over, but it gets darker towards its tail. Wait a second; I can see some yellow spots down its side. Look at those wings; each one has a dark tip, and there are smaller spots on the front edge of each of them, about half way along."

After a few minutes, I realised that I had seen this type of dragonfly before. The name of it was buried deep within my store of knowledge; all I had to find was the drawer in which it was kept, locate the key, and unlock it!

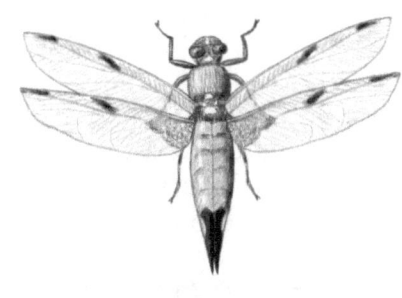

Four-spotted Chaser

Then, in flash it came to me. I was back in my childhood, holidaying in Cheshire and fishing on Lord Cholmondley's estate (with his kind permission, of course). His son, 'The young Lord,' as he was known, and I, had become quite friendly. It was he who had made me aware of this insect: the four-spotted chaser! He told me that the spots on the wings gave it its name and that's exactly how I managed to remember it. The scientific name, however, completely escaped me; perhaps I had never known it, but I was determined to look it up in my insect book when I arrived back at the *vardo*.

I continued to watch it for a few minutes as it dashed up and down the pond hunting its prey, other winged insects.

Then, just about as suddenly as it appeared, it shot off out of sight. I finished my packing and made my way back to the *vardo*, my welcoming little home on four wheels.

The fresh trout tasted so good, and I made quick work of my meal. I sat for a few moments on the *vardo* steps and reflected on just how lucky I was to live this life on the open road. I know so many people, for example, who have to make-do with shop-bought fish which is at least several days old. Here I was, with my meal eaten, and I had caught the fish not much more than an hour ago. Add to that the sight of the beautiful dragonfly, and now relaxing with a view over some of the best countryside that Britain had to offer; it made me feel like a king. I had no palace and no servants, but then I had the freedom to come and go as I pleased. I wouldn't change this life for the world.

Thoughtfully, I arose from my meditation and got back to practical things: breakfast dishes washed and stowed away, I harnessed Comma, lifted Raq aboard (I didn't want him to overdo things) and we got going.

Having opened the gate and manoeuvred the cumbersome *vardo* between the gateposts, I took a last look at the view.

"I really must return here some day," I thought, wistfully. It was simply lovely.

Finally, I pulled into the farm yard, once again to be greeted by the farmer and his wife.

"We're off," I stated, obviously.

"Please take these with our compliments," said the farmer's wife holding out a bag, which felt as though it contained bacon.

"Well, thank you so much," I replied, adding, "You've both been so kind to us. I just don't know how to repay you."

"That's easy," said the farmer, with a grin. "Next time you're on the radio, just mention Yew Tree Farm in one of your stories. That will let us know you haven't forgotten us; simple!"

"That's the least I can do," I chuckled.

I flicked Comma's reins, and with a creaking sound, the *vardo* began to move. We headed out of the gate, turned to the left, and our journey, recently so rudely interrupted, began again.

True to my word, some months later I was able to include a reference to the farm in one of my programmes. I also managed a little tale of a dragonfly, whose scientific name is *libellula quadrimaculata*, but I prefer to call it the four-spotted chaser!

Chapter 4

Cumberland at last!

Thankfully, the remainder of the journey was much less eventful and by the time the wheels of my old *vardo* crossed over the border into Cumberland, Raq was back to his old ways. There wasn't a rabbit along the lanes that was safe from his sensitive nose. No sooner had he scented one, than he gave chase. Fortunately for them, his legs were not as powerful as his sense of smell, and he had no success at all in catching one, but that wasn't for the want of trying!

Just before I reached the farm, to which my long and eventful journey had been leading, we pulled into the village of Glassonby, and now I was on familiar territory. We reached a junction in the lane; ahead was the small chapel and to the right the road that led to our final destination. However, we had a special call to make. I turned the bend, drove on for a short distance, then halted the *vardo* at the side of the road and crossed over to the gate into Midtown Farm.

The farmer's wife, Mrs Kidd, answered my knock on the farmhouse door. She greeted me with a, "Hello again, Romany; how nice to see you; come away in."

I followed her through into her neat little kitchen, where she kindly offered me a cup of tea, which I was glad to accept after so many long miles on the dusty road.

"Father's out in the fields," she told me, referring to her husband, John. "Arthur will be back from school shortly; he's been so looking forward to your visit," she concluded.

"I would have been here sooner, but for a little mishap," I smiled, and related the tale of the snake and our accident.

She agreed that Raq, and I, had been so lucky, and, in re-telling the story I realised just how serious the situation had been.

"The possible outcome just doesn't bear thinking about, Isabella," I said, reflectively.

As I was finishing my tea, I heard a familiar barking coming from the direction of the *vardo*.

"That's Raq's *friendly* bark," I told the Farmer's wife. "It always means that there's someone he knows, and I bet it's Arthur!"

Suddenly, the farmhouse door flew open and there stood a wiry boy of about twelve years of age.

"Arthur, old man, how are you?" I enquired. "It must be two years since I saw you last, and how you've grown!"

"Hello, Romany," he grinned. "I've been waiting for you. We've had a corncrake on our land this summer, but I think it's gone, now. It made me think of you when I first heard it; I wish you could have been here. It took me so long to find out what it was."

"Well done for finding out its name, Arthur," I congratulated him. "Did you get to see it?"

"No; I was really patient, just like you taught me, but it didn't matter what I did, I just couldn't spot it. It was really frustrating."

"Unfortunately, there are no guarantees when you watch wildlife," I sympathised. "You know, I've only seen *one*, in spite of all my years' birdwatching. In fact they're becoming quite rare, so I suppose I may never see another now."

Corncrake

After we had exchanged items of news, I excused myself, saying, "I must make my way up to Old Parks before it gets dark. The narrow gate makes for a tight turn into the Potter's farmyard, and I don't want to damage the *vardo* on the wall. Please give John my regards, and tell him I'll see him soon."

I crossed the farmyard, climbed onto the running board and with a, "Come along, Comma," the *vardo* trundled away.

There are many twists and turns along that narrow lane, and there's a small, difficult bridge to negotiate, but we managed it all without mishap. However, it's not a journey I'd like to repeat on a daily basis! Finally we reached a lane that branched off to our left. On the opposite side of the road was a sign, reading 'Old Parks Farm,' and we were almost at our journey's end.

No more than a quarter of a mile ahead lay the red-sandstone farmhouse and outbuildings. By now, the sun was beginning to set, and it bathed the buildings in a pinkish blush, enhancing their beauty. I called on Comma to halt for a moment, so that I could take in the sight. This was to be my home for the winter months, and a lovelier spot I could not imagine.

The farm lay on higher ground, and the slopes beneath it, where I knew the stream called 'Daleraven Beck' ran, were wooded and inviting. In the past, I had spent many a fine day watching birds and animals along the banks of the beck, and I intended to do the same again. I found it easy to slip into a daydream, recalling my unsuccessful escapades in trying to photograph the local fox whose home was there. But, with night rapidly falling, I urged on the horse, finally pulling-up at the gate into the yard.

I jumped down and was about to fling it open, when a voice said, "I knew it was you; I could hear your caravan creaking all the way up the lane!" and Joe Potter, the farmer, and incidentally, Arthur's uncle, strode into view.

After exchanging pleasantries, Joe held back the gate, while I guided Comma and the *vardo* through the narrow gap.

Joe showed me the best place to park, so that the movement of his cattle, or farming equipment, would not be impeded, although tomorrow I would move the *vardo* to where it belonged; out in the fields. Nevertheless, for now the yard was a convenient spot.

We went inside the farm and it was exactly as I remembered. The faint hiss of the oil lamps, which cast long, flickering shadows; the homely smell of Sallie's (Joe's wife) cooking; the friendly greeting from Judy, Joe's little dog. The gilt-lettered motto card mounted on the kitchen wall, announcing that, 'The glory of the home is hospitality,' summed-up Old Parks Farm for me. I had been made welcome here for many years; ever since I was introduced to the family by a mutual friend.

To my knowledge, there was never an occasion when a passing tramp was turned away. The kettle was always left to boil on the old black cast-iron kitchen range, and it seemed that Sallie could conjure-up a tasty meal at a moments' notice.

The lady herself appeared from another room, and gave me a big hug, saying, "I always look forward to your visits, Romany, and to think you're going to stay here long enough to have Christmas with us. Eee, we'll have a grand time of it!"

Over dinner, I told them about my exploits since my last visit, including, of course, my snake story. Their shocked response convinced me that this was a story to dine-out on for years to come!

They brought me up-to-date with farm and local happenings, finally asking me about my plans for the forthcoming months.

"I fully intend to photograph that fox," I informed them.

"He really out-foxed you the last time you were here!" Joe smiled, wryly.

"Very funny," I said. "This time I've brought my hiding-tent, and I have much more time to spare. I think I'll invite Arthur along to help."

I told them of my earlier visit to Midtown Farm, and my brief chat with the young lad.

The conversation went on long into the night. I particularly liked to hear Joe recount the tale of the Old Parks' ghost. Although I had heard it many times previously, I never tired of hearing it again.

Apparently, the present buildings replaced an earlier farm. It was in the old homestead that almost every morning the family would come downstairs to find that a corner of the large-rug was folded over. Even placing a heavy piano upon it had not prevented it happening! It was only when the farm was knocked down to make way for the current one, that a skeleton was found beneath the flagstones!

Although not easily unsettled, after hearing this story, I always felt a chill and tingling sensation on the back of my neck. Therefore, it was with some trepidation that I took an oil lamp, crossed the yard, and settled into the *vardo* for the night.

I had been in bed for no more than five minutes, and was just drifting off to sleep, when an unholy scream caused me to jump. It took a moment, or two, to remember that the call of a barn owl, sometimes known as the 'screech owl,' can have this effect on people. My heart was racing and it was at least another hour before I slipped into a deep slumber.

Barn owl

Midtown Farm

Arthur's mother, Isabella Kidd far right

Chapter 5

I survey my home

As usual, I arose early. Looking out from the open top-half of the *vardo* door, I could see through the gloom that already there was a light burning in the farmhouse kitchen. This meant that Joe was also up-and-about early, which, of course, is the lot of a farmer. However, rather than trouble him, I set-to making breakfast for Raq and myself. Comma was housed comfortably in the stable, along with Joe's working horses, and I would shortly make sure that she, too, was happy and fed.

I had no particular plans for the day, although I was of a mind to take a general walk around Joe's land. He always allowed me to have free-rein to come and go as I pleased, knowing I could be trusted to close all gates, not trample crops, and to take good care of his interests. People often forget that, when on farmland, we are simply guests at someone's place of work. The owner of a factory, for example, would be rather unhappy if we walked into the building and accidentally damaged his machinery, so why would we treat a farm and its land in a careless way?

With the plates stowed away, Comma happy in her stable, and Raq itching to be off, I crossed the yard and passed through a gate leading to the open fields. It was now fully light, and despite the lateness of the season, the rising sun over to my right held a promise of some warmth. All around me lay familiar territory. High Barn was out of sight beyond the shoulder of the hill. I could just make out the tops of the trees that I knew surrounded it. I would have to climb a good distance more before the buildings themselves would come into view, but that was for another day.

In the opposite direction, the fields sloped sharply away, only to rise quickly again to form a small hillock, perhaps a hundred and fifty yards distant. This was the spot where I loved to sit quietly and drink-in the beauty and the silence surrounding me. Those times were special, with only Raq for company. On many occasions, it was from that tiny hilltop that I gazed at its much larger sisters, perhaps some thirty, or more, miles away: the famous hills of the Northern Lake District. They were far craggier than the rounded and altogether gentler Fells beyond the Eden Valley, but, while I found a certain beauty in those majestic, and lofty peaks, my heart lay here. Although it would be impossible to manoeuvre the *vardo* onto that hillock, I thought that if I drove it beyond the yard and stayed on the track, I would be able to park-up with it in view; the next best thing. I resolved to move it that very afternoon.

Rabbit

Raq interrupted my reverie by giving a quick bark, and shooting off after a rabbit that had caught his eagle eye. I'm certain the local rabbits had become used to his antics, as they seemed to taunt him. I laughed aloud as bunny simply ran to the top of the hillock, gave a cheeky backward glance, and simply disappeared down a burrow.

Raq then ran back to me, tongue lolling, with his rapid-fire tail a blur, seeming to say, "Nearly got him, this time, Romany." What he had forgotten was that he had tried at least a hundred times before!

"Come on, old man," I chuckled, adding, "If we stay here much longer, you won't be fit to do any walking; the rabbits will have exhausted you," and I set off along the track leading away from both the farm and the hillock. Ahead lay a wood, which in springtime, is a carpet of blue as the bluebells nod their heads in the breeze. I recalled the faint smell of hyacinths from past visits, the bluebell being part of the hyacinth family. No such luck at this time of year, of course.

As we came abreast of the wood, we disturbed half-a-dozen wood pigeons, whose initial wing-claps sounded almost like pistol shots as they rose from their perch and flew away from us.

"Mole's been busy," I announced, to nobody in particular, as I surveyed the dark mounds of earth scattered across the field in front of us. I always pity the poor gardener who, proud of his bowling-green-like lawn, awakes one morning to find that a mole has turned his prized possession into a miniature lunar landscape.

Although moles are plentiful, because of their subterranean habits they are scarcely seen. Most people go through life seeing only dead ones that have been tied to fences after the local mole-catcher has been busy. Very few people are lucky enough to see a live mole above ground, and when they do it's only for a moment as it sniffs the air with its pink, wet, piggy nose, and then disappears. It is a case of one being in the right place at the right time, with a large dose of luck thrown in. Sometimes he is affectionately known as 'the man in the black-velvet jacket,' but there's not too much affection from proud gardeners whose prize lawns have had this little chap's attention!

Mole

I wandered on through a shallow valley, the almost bare trees on my left looking for all the world like skeletal fingers, contrasting darkly against the bright sky. A gentle breeze caused them to shimmer, bringing life to them and adding to the illusion. An occasional flutter of wings broke the spell, bringing me down to earth.

As the sides of the valley gradually flattened out, I saw ahead of me the ruins of a castle, surrounded by trees. The ground became rather muddy, trampled by the hooves of many cattle, seeking water from what remained of the castle moat. Because I had been here before, I knew that so thick were the trees, that the castle would be all but invisible in the height of summer.

Drawing closer to the remains of the large tower, it made me sad that memories of the past glory of this home had been lost with the passing of time. It struck me that the all-powerful hand of man, which had once transformed this quiet, secluded location into a bustling place, was capable of making only temporary changes; Mother Nature had once more reclaimed her own. Trees had taken root where stately war-horses had pranced; thick, spongy layers of moss clung to every stone, giving the appearance that the castle was a living thing that had sprouted from the earth; rooks had colonised the invading trees, and their mournful calls gave the whole place an air of melancholy. Now I'm not a superstitious person, but I would not like to spend a night alone in that spot; too much had happened there for it to ever feel a happy place.

The air suddenly felt cold, making me shiver for a moment. I then turned on my heel, whistled to Raq, and strode purposefully back the way I had come.

I kept up a brisk pace, putting distance between me and the ruin, although with every step, my rational thoughts told me I was being foolish, I would not have wished to remain a minute longer.

As my mind settled, moving the *vardo* before nightfall became uppermost in my thoughts. So it was, that by walking at least twice as fast as on my outward journey, we soon arrived back on the farm.

Joe, who was already in the yard, greeted me as I appeared from between the farmhouse and the adjacent barn.

"Hello, Romany! I hadn't expected you back so early."

"I very much want to get the *vardo* out of your way and onto that high ground along the track, assuming it's alright with you?"

"Of course it is," he replied. "In fact, I'll lend a hand as you drive it through the gate," he offered, adding, "It can be a bit tricky when I take the cart through, and I do it nearly every day."

I went to the stable and fetched Comma. After I'd harnessed her, I gently coaxed her backwards into the *vardo* shafts, which Joe obligingly held up at just the right height.

Once she was secured, I climbed onto the running board and urged her on.

"Come on, Comma, lass," I told her, and with a lurch we crossed the yard. Joe ran ahead and opened the gate, while we gingerly made our way through.

I deliberately held her back, as she was excited and wanted to trot. This would have been disastrous, as the track was by no means even; many small rocks littered our path, threatening to overbalance us, or even break a wheel rim.

However, after a few anxious minutes I pulled her to the right, off the track and onto quite a level, grassy bank. Although I wanted the door of the *vardo* to face my little hillock, I didn't want to make things too complicated. I unhitched the horse, led her back into her stable, and returned to the *vardo*, where Joe awaited me. Together, we manhandled my mobile home into a more suitable position.

"I wouldn't want to be a horse," Joe remarked. "That small manoeuvre was quite enough for me!" he laughed.

"Well thank you for your help," I said. "It's not something I like to do alone. The *vardo* weighs close to a ton."

Joe strode off back to his work, and I busied myself making the site comfortable. From the *vardo* I brought the *chitty*, that is, the long iron rods I use to suspend my kettle and cooking pots over my fire. I gathered a number of large stones and made them into a circle beneath the tripod. The stones would contain the twigs and small logs for my *yog,* or fire.

Joe had kindly offered me free use of the contents of his woodshed, which was just as well, as dry timber was in short supply on the ground.

I had an early supper, before darkness fell, and spent the last half-hour of daylight gazing across the small valley to the hillock, the woods beyond, and to the valley in which ran the beck. Although it was out of sight, the gentle, tinkling sound was a constant reminder of its presence.

I went to bed a happy man. The fields, woods, streams and valleys that I loved lay before me, and a little farther off, my beloved Fells. My plan for the next few months was to *have* no plan, just like my Gypsy ancestors before me. What more could I possibly want?

Chapter 6

The school

A few relatively uneventful and relaxing weeks passed by. Raq and I had become used to our surroundings and I had settled into a daily routine of cooking, walking and birdwatching, which was pleasant in itself, but not overly challenging. With the changing season, the days and nights had become sufficiently cold as to prevent our eating outside the *vardo*, and my morning 'cuppa' on the *vardo* step was a distant memory.

Early one evening, with the long shadows falling, Raq was dozing near to the warm stove, when I felt the *vardo* shake slightly as somebody ascended the steps. Before I could reach the door, there came a gentle tap, and a small voice saying, "Are you there, Romany? It's me, Arthur."

I opened the door, and there, bathed in the glow from the oil lamps stood young Arthur Kidd.

I greeted him with, "I haven't seen you for weeks, Arthur! Come along inside."

Raq, rather belatedly, gave a little bark, and made a fuss of him as I beckoned him over to one of the bench seats and sat down opposite him.

After we exchanged pleasantries, and I had enquired about the health of his family, he came to the point of his visit.

"I told my teacher, Miss Sidney, that you were staying on the farm, and she asked if you would like to come to the school to talk to us about your adventures. I said I'd come up here and ask you and then let her know."

"Which school is it?" I enquired.

"It's Kirkoswald School. We all listen to your programmes on the wireless."

"Well, Arthur, I'd love to. Do you know when you'd like me there, because I'd need to do some preparation?"

"Miss Sidney said that Friday of next week would be fine," he announced.

"Good. That gives me almost two weeks, then. Shall we say two o'clock?"

He simply nodded, grinning from ear to ear.

After he'd had a cup of tea, he left for home, taking with him one of my lamps to light his way down the dark lane. I watched the yellow light swaying as he followed the track towards the farmyard, finally disappearing as he passed through the gate and the buildings obscured my view.

I already had some idea of what I would talk about when I visited the school, but I wanted to make it lively and interesting, so I would need to gather a few things together before then.

I spent the intervening days collecting items with which to illustrate my talk: a feather, some moss, and so on. I had decided to use the title of my radio programme, as the name of my talk: 'Out with Romany.'

When the day dawned, I was ready. I took an early lunch and then strode-off across the fields in the direction of Kirkoswald, about an hour's walk away.

On my route, I again passed the castle, which had made me feel so peculiar some weeks before. This time I felt no particular emotion as I passed by, my mind on the forthcoming talk. Raq, too, was occupied with other thoughts, as he eagerly sniffed the ground for traces of birds and animals, his nose providing him with a commentary on all of the goings-on of the past week.

'If only I could be like him, the effort I put into tracking wildlife would be made so much easier,' I thought, as I observed him. 'I would see a lot more, too!'

He never walked in a straight line, continually weaving from side-to-side. As he lost a trail, he moved around until he found it again, or located something completely new that took over his interest. He would occasionally stop, obviously finding something slightly more fascinating to absorb his thoughts.

The track we were following eventually came out onto a lane, where we turned left on the outskirts of the village. The houses and walls were a rather attractive rust-colour, being built from sandstone, and the weak afternoon sun seemed to enhance their glow.

I walked on through the small square, following the directions Arthur had given me. He had been very clear in his instructions, and, turning left and climbing a hill, I found myself at the gates of the school, just as he said I would. Before entering, I crossed the road to gain an impression of the building. It, too, was made of the same material as the entire village, and blended in very nicely with the uniform nature of Kirkoswald. It looked a natural part of the landscape, with a very homely feel to it. I could imagine a welcoming place, where children wanted to learn, and enjoyed what they did.

I walked back to the door and tried the handle. It opened easily, giving a reassuring creak, as every heavy, wooden door should. I stood for a moment in the slightly darkened passageway while my eyes adjusted to the lower light level, and I found myself in a Victorian building. Immediately, my senses took me back to my old school in Rhyl, North Wales; there was that familiar smell of floor polish, of school dinners; the faint classroom sounds of children talking, laughing, singing.

My thoughts were interrupted by, "Welcome to Kirkoswald School, Romany. I'm Mr Shaw, headmaster," adding, "I'm delighted Miss Sidney has organised this. We are all looking forward so much to your talk."

"Well, it's very good of you to invite me," I responded. "There's a very friendly feel to your school," I said.

"I'm sure Arthur has told you that most of the children listen to your programme, and, I'd like to add, so do I! This will be a real treat for us all."

He bent down to pat the dog.

"This must be the famous Raq," he said, mischievously adding, "I wonder exactly who is more famous; you, or he?"

"Oh, it's him every time," I chuckled. "In fact, would you mind if we kept him out-of-sight? I'd like to introduce him in a particular way, if that's possible?"

"He'll be safe in my office, if that's alright with you?" Mr Shaw suggested.

"As long as I leave my jacket for him to guard, he'll be absolutely fine," I answered.

He led the way and I hung my coat on the back of a chair, ordering Raq to jump up and 'stay,' which he immediately did. The sorrowful eyes said, 'Can't I come with you?' but he knew his duty and remained in position. We went into the small school hall, where, seated cross-legged on the floor, were approximately fifty children. The teachers were there as well, including Miss Sidney. Obviously all the classes had come, not just Arthur's.

They all stood up as we entered and gave a round of applause, which I found very flattering. The headmaster introduced me:

"Today, children, we are privileged to have with us a very famous radio broadcaster and author: Romany of the BBC." Another round of applause followed.

"Romany has brought his Gypsy caravan to Cumberland to spend the winter. We have all heard so much about it, and his adventures, and now we are going to hear him speak first-hand. This is a day you will remember for all of your lives!"

I started to feel a bit uncomfortable with such a glowing introduction, so I was glad to hear Mr Shaw say, "And now, children, it is time to go, 'Out with Romany,'" which was exactly how the BBC announcer introduced my programme.

My, "Good afternoon, everyone," was greeted with a well-timed response of, "Good afternoon, Romany."

I looked down upon a lake of smiling, upturned faces. One, or two of the pupils were craning their necks, and I suspected I knew why; they were looking for Raq. I said nothing, as I had a plan up my sleeve!

For half an hour or so, the children sat seemingly spell-bound as I told them of the adventures I had had seeking out and watching various birds and animals. I tried to encourage them to take more notice of the birds that came to their gardens, and I did a few sketches of some birds they might try to spot.

"Look out for this little chap, for example," I said, making a rapid charcoal caricature of a wren.

"He's *almost* the smallest bird in this country, and he's quite secretive as he skulks around under bushes and in crevices, on the look out for food.

But......his voice is really *enormous* for his tiny size. You will, although you may not realise it, have heard this little bird many times," I continued. "When he's alarmed at something he sets up a sharp and rapid ticking sound, but when he bursts into song, why, then you will find it hard to believe how so much sound can come from such a wee little creature."

I did my best to imitate the song for them – "twiddle, tee,tee,tee,tttttttttttt tweee." That got a laugh, but one girl in her excitement called out, "I've heard that!"

"Let Romany go on, please," interjected the headmaster. "You can all ask questions at the end.

"Indeed you can," I echoed.

Knowing that there were becks in the surrounding area from which the children came to Kirkoswald school, and, of course, the magnificent River Eden, I next suggested that they might like to look out for the dipper, which I rapidly sketched for them.

"He likes to alight on a boulder or over-hanging branch by the water, and then do his little dance," I said.

I then got hoots of laughter as I demon-strated, doing a series of deep knee bends.

"From a distance he looks black and white, but up close you can see that his colouring is a bit more interesting than that. He looks a bit like a tubby waiter in his black suit and white shirt front; or," I added mischievously, "like a vicar with too big a collar!"

There was more laughter.

And so I continued until I felt it was time to give them the opportunity to meet Raq. I nodded to the headmaster who opened the door out to the corridor so that my voice would carry to the office where I knew the obedient dog would not have moved from his chair, but would be waiting patiently and expectantly.

"Would you like to see Raq?" I asked; and that was the cue Raq had been waiting for. He came bounding in to great cheering.

"*Kushto jukal*," I said, fondling him. I then sent him off to greet the children. The pupils loved it and Raq revelled in all the attention.

Eventually I called Raq to come and sit at my feet and I invited question.

It was the same enthusiastic lass who had called out about the wren whose hand shot up first.

"Yes, my dear," I invited.

"You seemed to be speaking to your dog in a foreign language," she said.

I smiled and said, "I was indeed. I often talk to Raq using the *Romani* language. *Kushto jukal* means good dog."

"Oooh, oooh, me, Romany,me," called out an excited lad who seemed to be trying to push his hand right up to the ceiling in his attempt to attract my attention.

"Yes," I said smiling at him. I thought if he didn't have his say he might burst!

"*Vardo* is a Gypsy word, isn't it? That's what you call your caravan," he blurted out.

"You are right," I replied, "it is and I do!"

I was relieved that the next question actually got us back to wildlife! I am proud of my Gypsy ancestry, and I know it fascinates a lot of my listeners and readers, but it is a love of Nature that I most wish to promote.

Eventually the headmaster drew things to a close by saying, "Just one more question and then we must let Romany go."

"If the wren is *nearly* the smallest bird, what is actually the smallest?" This question had come from Arthur and it seemed fitting that it should be so as he had been instrumental in bringing me to the school.

"In this country the smallest birds are the goldcrest and the firecrest. Both the same size, just three and a half inches long, but they have slightly different streaks of orange over the crown," I answered. There is actually a bit more to it than that but I thought that answer was sufficient since the afternoon was wearing on, and I guessed the staff would want a bit of lesson time left before the children went home.

After Mr Shaw had thanked me and the children had shown their appreciation with thunderous clapping, I began to make my way out of the school hall, promising that I would have a set of my books sent to the school to go in their library.

"Remember me to your parents, Thomas," I said as I passed a boy rather younger than Arthur.

Looking as if I had just performed a miracle he said, "How do you know my name?"

"Your parents put a family photo for me in with their Christmas card last year," I replied.

"So you know my parents, then?" Thomas responded.

"I do indeed. Why, I *married* them some years ago at Kirkbride Chapel before they moved to Gamblesby.

"Gosh. Wait till I tell them," he said excitedly.

"Tell them I shall call in to see them some time," I said as I left.

Gamblesby is a village near the foot of the Fells, and a plan was beginning to form in my mind, but it was a plan that would have to wait for Spring weather.

Arthur and his Family

Arthur is on the left

Chapter 7

I encounter the helm wind

On several occasions when visiting the farm I had heard Joe talk of a local phenomenon known as the 'helm wind.' He became almost reverential when discussing it, dropping his voice to a low tone and speaking as though it were some great secret.

At first, I knew nothing about it, but, on questioning him, my curiosity was aroused to the point that I once visited the library in Penrith to carry out some research. It was there that I learned that it always occurs on the mountain slope opposite to the side on which there is rain. The wind travels upward on the wet side, losing its moisture in the form of rain, and then climbs over the summit, dropping sharply down 2,000 feet on the other side. It is usually quite a warm north-easterly wind, but it is extremely powerful and damaging. Whilst these types of winds happen all over the world, particularly in the Alps, in England it appears on the south-western slopes of Cross Fell, which lie behind Old Parks Farm.

Joe told me that when it happens, it can last for several days, and is so severe that it usually causes considerable damage to trees and buildings. He went on to describe the special cloud that appears above the Fell, giving an early warning of the onset of the wind. The very word 'helm' is short for 'helmet,' describing exactly how the cloud sits on the mountaintop, looking just like a hat! This cloud builds-up in a line along Cross Fell, and is given the name of the 'Helm bar.'

Despite many visits to the farm, I still had not experienced the helm wind. Of course, many would say that to have an ambition to witness such a potentially destructive force is foolhardy. However, I possess an inquisitive mind when it comes to our natural world, and not everything in nature is pleasant.

Several weeks passed following my visit to the school, and Arthur had popped by to see me on several occasions. On each trip, he was guaranteed to have brought a feather, a scrap of fur, or an old and disused bird's nest for identification. I could see that *his* interest in nature was growing, which I found very rewarding.

With his parents' permission, I had arranged that we would make an early-morning visit to the earth of the local fox that I previously mentioned. So, one Friday afternoon, with plans made for the coming Saturday, to avoid the need for Arthur to be up for school, I bustled about the *vardo* getting things ready. From the cupboards, I produced my binoculars and a spare pair for the young lad, the thermos flask for a hot drink, Raq's lead (he was coming, too, as I knew he would behave if I told him to), and the many other things a naturalist needs for a field trip.

It was arranged that Arthur would stay with me on the Friday night, so that we could be up and out before dawn. That morning, I had pitched my big, ex-army tent, in which I would sleep, leaving the youngster to the comfort of the *vardo*. Winter was coming on, and I wasn't looking forward to a night under canvas, but it was for one night only, and I had slept-out under worse conditions in the past.

It was growing dusk and I went to fetch firewood from Joe's wood store, when I glanced up at the fellside.

"Well I never," I said to Raq, who simply wagged his stumpy tail. Lying over the crest of Cross Fell was an unusual, and highly distinctive, band of cloud. It could only mean one thing – the helm wind.

I crossed the yard and knocked on the door. Sallie answered after a few moments.

She greeted me with, "Now then, Romany; there's no need for you to knock. You're more welcome here than most. Come away inside."

"I won't, thanks, Sallie, if it's all the same to you. I've got Arthur Kidd coming to stay tonight and I want to get on. I noticed that strange cloud over on Cross

Fell and wondered if it might be the helm bar, so I thought I would ask an expert."

"Well, I wouldn't say I'm an expert," she blushed, "but I would say it is. I do hope Joe spots it in time. He's working up at High Barn today and the wind fair roars over the tops just there."

I left her and headed back towards the *vardo*, noticing the freshening breeze ruffling Raq's fur. Looking up at the hillside on which lay High Barn, I was relieved to see Joe making his way down the track, although he was a good half-mile away. At least I knew he would be safe for the night. I waited until he appeared to be looking in my direction and then gave an exaggerated wave. He raised his arm to acknowledge my greeting and I carried on to my little wooden home.

Arthur duly arrived at six o'clock sharp, as agreed. Already, I had a tasty meal stewing on the fire outside, although the strong gusts of wind had made the cooking time twice as long.

"Eee, that smells reet grand," he grinned, eying the pot.

"I expect a growing lad like you could manage a plateful?" I answered.

He shyly smiled saying, "Yes, please, Romany," whilst patting Raq's head in greeting.

It being far too cold to sit outside, I told him to go in and light the oil lamps. I soon followed him in with the stewpot.

After our meal, for which he complemented me, we set-to and washed up.

"I've never had a meal cooked on an open fire," said the boy. "It tastes a bit smoky-like, but very nice."

"I always try to cook outside, if the weather's alright," I told him. "The fire does make things smoky, and it takes some getting used to, when even a cup of tea tastes of smoke, but I've grown to love it."

"What happens when the weather's bad, then? Do you have only cold food?" he enquired.

"Heavens, no!" I told him. "There's the indoor stove, too. It's not quite the same, of course, but at least it means I can cook."

"And I thought it was just for heating the *vardo*," he smiled.

"Did you notice the cloud before you left home?" I asked him, changing the subject.

He shook his head.

"Well, I'm not sure we'll be looking for foxes tomorrow," I informed him. "I think we're in for a helm wind."

His eyes opened like saucers and he blurted out, "Ooh! Do you think we'll be safe, Romany?"

"Safe as houses," I confidently replied, while not feeling quite as certain inside.

We relaxed on the cushioned *vardo* benches and I told him tales of bird and animal watching. He said how much his classmates had enjoyed my talk, and that they had been set a project to draw, or paint, an illustration from one of my stories. Miss Sidney wondered if I might judge the competition, as there was to be a special winner's prize.

"Please tell her I'd be glad to," I told him.

As the night drew on, I noticed that the heavy *vardo* rocked every now and again, as though pushed by some giant hand. I felt glad that I had chosen not to park the caravan beneath any trees; who knows whether some mighty elm might choose this night to drop a large overhanging bough upon my roof!

Finally, at around 9.30, I announced, "I'm turning in, Arthur. Let's get your bed made up."

He glanced around him and announced, "I can't see any bed, Romany."

"Of course you can't;" I confirmed, "we have to get the planks out from under the end bench and lay them across those rails," and I pointed to two pieces of wood screwed onto either wall.

It was the work of only a few minutes to place the planks in position, lay the mattress upon them, and make his bed.

"I suspect Raq will want to come with me, Arthur. Will you be alright on your own?"

"Yes, Romany, I'll be fine. I slept in our barn one really hot night."

I left him on board and walked across the grass to the tent. The wind was now very strong indeed and the storm lamp I was carrying swung so violently as to be of little use. I undid the flap to enter the tent and it was immediately torn from my grasp, making a loud, slapping sound as the wind whipped it back against the tent wall. I struggled to fasten it behind me and became aware of the powerful rustling of the fabric as it was buffeted by the rising gale.

I climbed into bed, but soon realised that the prospect of any sleep was highly unlikely.

As the night wore slowly on, I observed a pattern: the wind would momentarily die to a whisper, only to be followed by a roar like an express train passing through a station, at which point my old tent would bend alarmingly under the strain. Fearing that it might not survive the night, I made ready to move out at a moment's notice and left the lamp burning to ensure a quick exit. I really envied Raq's ability to sleep through the storm. Also, I was concerned about Arthur. The *vardo* is of considerable weight, so it was not that I feared it might topple over, but more that the boy would be cowering, afraid.

It was around two o'clock in the morning, with the tempest at its height, that I decided enough was enough.

"Come on, old man," I said to Raq, raising my voice almost to a shout to make myself heard. As with all dogs, he was instantly alert, his tail trembling at the prospect of a walk!

"Not now, Raq; the only place we're walking to is the *vardo*," I bawled.

Taking real care, I gingerly undid the tent door and squeezed through a small crack, with Raq following. I hastily fastened it up, and battled through the powerful wind towards where I knew the *vardo* to be. Twice I was all but bowled over, leaning forward at a sharp angle to resist the terrible force pressing against me. Raq, too, found our short journey to be a difficult one, his long, cocker spaniel ears flowing behind him like streamers, mouth wide open, tongue lolling.

I found I simply could not walk up the steps and was blown to the ground, luckily only from the first tread. Prudence got the better of me, and I ascended in an undignified manner on my hands and knees, hoisting up my little companion by his strong, leather collar.

I knew the door would fly open, so I took a firm grip with both hands, slowly turning the handle until I could step inside.

Fully expecting to see Arthur shivering under a blanket, I raised the wick on the lamp to get more light. Imagine my surprise when I found his bed was empty! Where on earth could he be? Believe me, there is nowhere to hide in the *vardo*!

Thoughts flashed through my mind: 'He's gone out to find me in the tent and got lost;' 'He became frightened and has tried to walk home.'

I decided I needed help; it was pointless calling out his name in this noise; I could hardly hear myself speak, let alone be heard over any distance.

As best I could, I ran to the farm. At least I attempted to run. Even though I was forcing my legs like a sprinter, I wasn't even managing a proper walking pace.

Eventually, I found myself hammering at the kitchen door. After a few minutes, a lamp was lit and the door opened a small way; it was Joe.

"Oh, Romany, I'm glad you're safe," he said. "Come in out of the wind."

"No Joe, I can't. Arthur's missing. I left him in bed in the *vardo*, but he's gone; he could be anywhere. We *have* to find him!"

Just then, a small voice piped up from inside the kitchen, "I'm here, Romany!"

I went inside, mightily relieved. He told me how he hadn't been able to sleep because of the noise and the constant rocking of the *vardo* had made him feel sick. So, he had come to the farm, where his Uncle Joe and Aunt Sallie had made him at home.

"Well, I'm so glad that you're alright, Arthur," I told him. "That must have been a real experience for you?"

"It's certainly taught me one thing," he replied.

"What's that?"

"I'm never going in the Navy," he laughed.

And he never did. When it was time to join the services, he decided that the air force was a much better option!

When, a week or so later, it came to judging the work produced by Arthur's class, I was very impressed with the standard of the work which had been produced. The pieces did not have the pupils' names on them but rather they were numbered, only the teacher knowing to whom the work belonged. I was glad of this because the winning piece turned out to be Arthur's, and it could otherwise have looked rather like favouritism. Arthur was delighted with his success.

Chapter 8

The changing season

The nights had become increasingly cold and the landscape stark and bare during the time I had been on the farm. Trees that I remembered from earlier spring and summer visits as large, and mushrooming with lush foliage, appeared visibly to have shrunk to mere skeletons. What little grass was left had taken on an almost grey appearance and was limp and lifeless, offering little nourishment to Joe's cattle. Consequently, the fields surrounding the farm were scattered with hay to supplement their feed, looking unnatural, and somewhat like snipped hair on the hairdresser's floor.

However, although far less apparent, life went on amongst the wild creatures that populated the locality. Indeed, one morning while washing my breakfast dishes, some movement seen through the *vardo* window attracted my attention. I had expected that I would see these winter visitors at some point and now that I knew they had arrived I was anxious to show them to Arthur.

It being a Friday, when he would not be at school the following day, I decided to combine a trip to the village shop with a visit to Midtown Farm, to leave a message for him to join me at the *vardo* first thing on Saturday.

Mrs Kidd answered my knock, with a, "Hello Romany. We don't see you often enough; come on in."

I answered with, "I hope you don't mind Raq joining us?" adding, "He's a little muddy from the fields."

"Bless you, Romany," she laughed. "My father was a farmer and I married a farmer; muddy dogs are a way of life. I only hope that Joe doesn't know you've pinched some of his mud from Old Parks!"

"Well, I'd prefer you didn't tell him, Isabella," I chuckled.

She asked me to sit down by her roaring fire, which was a most welcome respite from the chill beyond the door. I was delighted when she offered me a slice of pork pie, as I'd experienced the delights of her home-cooking on other occasions. Just as I could have predicted, it was moist and full of flavour, and was washed down with a cup of tea, made with water from the old black kettle that rested at the side of the fire.

Our conversation ranged from the selling-price of cattle, to the rising cost of winter feed, by way of how Arthur was progressing at school, and finally arriving at the perennial British topic of the weather!

"What sort of winter would a farmer's wife reckon we're going to have?" I enquired.

"Judging by the amount of berries on the quickthorn, it'll be a hard one," she answered.

"Quickthorn? That's not something with which I'm familiar."

"Oh, I'm sorry; you'll know it as hawthorn. Sometimes we call it 'May' – you know, 'ne'er cast a clout 'til May is out.'"

I nodded.

Hawthorn

"Some folk think the saying means: 'don't stop using your winter clothes until the month of May is over', but it doesn't. It means wait until the May blossom is out. Quickthorn's a canny bush; it only blossoms when the weather turns warmer, so that means it's alright to shed some clothes."

"So, are you saying that a large crop of berries means there will be a harsh winter," I asked.

"That's what my old Dad used to say, and he was right, more often than not."

"In that case I should stock my larder, by way of insurance," I smiled

Saying goodbye at the door, I also left the message for Arthur. Raq and I turned right out of the yard and onto the lane, which eventually led back to our camp. Although he is a well-behaved dog, and would never do anything to disgrace himself, I knew he had hankered after a piece of the delicious pork pie that I had enjoyed by that cosy fireside. Although he had lain in front of the hearth, and appeared to fall asleep, I knew him too well. His ears remained pricked for the slightest indication that I might smuggle him a morsel, but that wasn't to be. However, imagine his delight when on arriving back at the *vardo*, I slipped from my 'poacher's' pocket a beef bone wrapped in newspaper that Mrs Kidd had passed to me, with a quiet, "Here; this is for Raq."

As he busied himself gnawing away at his new-found treasure, I lit the oil lamps and settled down for the evening.

He must have enjoyed the bone so much that, the following morning, just as dawn was breaking, Arthur arrived at the *vardo* steps without awakening the slumbering dog, which was a very unusual event.

"He's quiet," was the boy's first observation.

On hearing his voice, though, Raq was up and greeting the lad with excited yelps.

"Mum said you had something new to show me, Romany. I can't think what it might be."

"Well, it was something I saw yesterday; it's a bird, or should I say two birds. For me, when I see them, it confirms that winter has arrived."

"Do they migrate, then, Romany?"

I confirmed that they were migrants and we spoke at length about that seasonal miracle, where animals and birds made long journeys to places that better suited their needs, whether that was somewhere to breed, or to find water and food, or simply to avoid harsher weather conditions.

Several times he pressed me to tell him what I had seen, but I steadfastly refused. Instead, I offered him a challenge. When, and if, I saw the birds again, I would ask him to identify what it was that was different about the two species; what it was that made them unlike other, similar British birds. I called it 'Arthur's Observation Challenge.'

An hour or two of pleasant chat passed by as we strolled around the fields, when thirty yards away I saw a flock of starling-sized birds alight in a hedge.

"This could be what we're waiting for," I said.

Raising my binoculars to my eyes, I could clearly see a small number of the flock, the rest being hidden from view. Immediately, I knew this was what we were waiting for.

"Arthur," – I paused, for effect – "The challenge begins," I announced, passing him the binoculars.

He scanned the hedge and after a moment said, in a despondent voice, "They're just song thrushes. They don't migrate – they stay with us all year round."

"Look again, old man," I replied. "I grant you they are about the same size, and actually they are from the thrush family, but they are different birds altogether. Look at them in detail and tell me what you see."

"They seem as though they're eating the berries."

"Yes, they are; well done. Now take a look at the birds themselves."

"Well, it has a grey head and back, with speckles on its chest."

"Good start, Arthur. Can you see anything about its eye area?"

Yes, I can see a stripe that runs across the top of its eye; a song thrush doesn't have that."

"Well spotted, Arthur. Actually, the song thrush does have a marking above the eye, but it's not nearly as obvious as on that bird. Is there anything you notice about the speckles on its chest?"

"Well it's difficult to be sure at this distance, but it looks as though they could be 'V' shaped, and I don't think that's the same as the song thrush."

"Your young eyesight is excellent," I complimented him. "Just find me one more difference and we can look at the other species."

"Other species? I think there's only one," then suddenly he said, "Wait, one of them's got some red underneath its wing. Do you think it's injured?"

"No, no," I reassured him, "It's not hurt – that's just the other bird and you've already found a key distinguishing feature. You can describe it a little more in just a moment. Concentrate on that final difference in the other one."

"I think it must be its brown wings – they're almost the colour of a chestnut."

"Fantastic, Arthur," I enthused. "Grey head and rump, with a strong, light-coloured eye stripe. Chestnut-coloured wings and 'V'-shaped breast markings. You've seen your first fieldfare!"

Fieldfare

"So, on to that other bird. Apart from the red area below the wings, what else can you see that makes it different from a song thrush?"

"It's also got an eye-stripe, and one that runs from the bottom of its beak to its neck."

"Yes, its face-markings are altogether much more obvious. Can you see any-thing else that's different?"

"Its beak seems to be yellowier, but it's hard to be sure because I can't see a song thrush to compare it to. It's hard to remember the strength of a colour."

"That's why it's important to have a good bird-guide – you know the kind of book I keep in the *vardo*. You can make a comparison that way. Although I have to say you're spot-on – the beak *is* yellowier. So, I told you that the first bird is a fieldfare, now you guess the name of this one."

After some hesitation, he said, "A hedgefare, maybe?"

"Well, no, but it's a good try. It's something to do with what's different about it."

"Is it the red colouring?" was his question. I simply nodded.

"Redfare?"

"Where is the red marking?"

"By its wing," he answered.

"So, that makes it a …….." I paused, inviting a response.

"*Redwing!*" he shouted, joyously.

Immediately, the flock of birds rose in the air and were gone.

Redwings

"That's three things you've learned today, Arthur, my lad," I remarked, as we found our way back to the caravan.

"Surely you mean two things, Romany: what a redwing and a fieldfare look like."

"Ah, but the third lesson is that you can't be a successful wildlife observer if you shout!"

He gave a wry smile as we crossed the fields to the *vardo*, where we warmed ourselves with a welcome cup of tea.

Chapter 9

Christmas Eve at the *vardo*

It was Christmas Eve and a frosty morning had dawned. The previous night, I had made up my mind to make the *vardo* look more festive. Consequently, soon after breakfast, Raq and I took a leisurely stroll across the fields to the woods, where, on an expedition a few days earlier, I had spotted some holly that had been untouched by the local birds.

Entering the wood, we followed the track that ran beneath the overarching canopy. Glancing upwards, the tightly woven branches above us looked for all the world like the fine masonry that you might see in a cathedral. After travelling only a few yards, I was struck by the hush that had descended around us. Not a woodland bird was calling, no rabbits were scampering, the normally vocal pheasants had vanished; all was silent.

We arrived in the clearing where I had previously encountered the holly, and I was pleasantly surprised to see just how bright the scarlet berries looked against the dark green foliage.

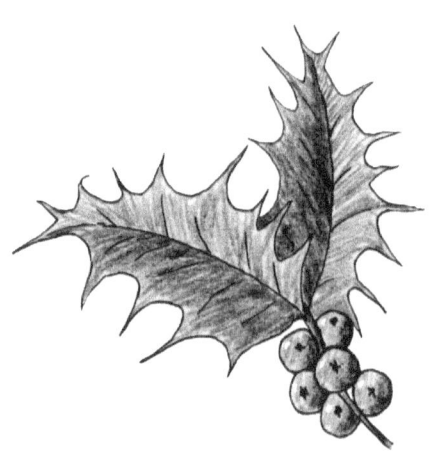

"They're like little lights," I whispered to Raq, who wagged his tail. I say 'whispered,' as it felt inappropriate to use a normal speaking voice in the hallowed silence of the glade.

Using my trusty pocket-knife, I removed a dozen, or so, branches, which I then tied together with some baling-twine I'd begged from Joe.

"Before we go, let's sit for a few moments," I said to Raq.

Placing my knapsack on the ground, I lowered myself onto it. Looking around me, the peace and utter silence of that winter scene was almost tangible. The heavy frost lying coating the ground caught the rays of the watery sun, and it sparkled like fine diamonds. Our breath steamed like Sallie's farmhouse kettle in the cold, crisp air.

"What a fine day to be alive," I muttered; and that summed-up just how I felt.

Raq, too, seemed to be subdued by the atmosphere of that muted place. He would usually be running about, letting his nose tell him tales of the creatures that had passed by: the weasel seeking a meal; the rabbit avoiding the weasel.

A sudden raucous cackle lifted us both from our reverie, and a cock pheasant shot across the track before us, hotly pursued by a fox! The animal looked neither right, nor left and disappeared into the undergrowth just as quickly as he'd appeared.

I gripped Raq's collar, as he jumped to his feet, ready, in turn, to chase the fox.

"No fox hunting for you, old boy," I laughed. "I still have to photograph him," reminding myself of my earlier promise to Arthur.

After Raq had calmed down, I got to my feet, feeling stiff from sitting idle in the cold. Trimming some ivy branches soon warmed me, and I added them to the holly I'd collected.

"The *vardo* will look festive," I told the dog, who was far more interested in sniffing around the area where the fox had crossed the glade. His tail was wagging furiously, as he encountered the pungent scent of fox.

"Come along Raq," I called to him, as I returned down the track. Reluctantly, he obeyed, and came to heel.

We were soon in the open fields again, and headed back to the *vardo*, where, after a spot of lunch, I made preparations to decorate the inside.

Weaving ivy around each holly branch, I made garlands that I would pin high on the *vardo* walls.

After an hour's work, the *vardo* looked a Christmas delight. The berries added a splash of colour to the largely cream interior. The finishing touch would come as dusk fell and I lit the oil lamps. I relished the cosy glow they would bring and looked forward to evening.

Glancing through one of the windows, I could see Joe, and his faithful border collie, fetching down the sheep from the hillside above. I understood that he would want them to be closer to the farm the following morning. Although the majority of us would take a holiday on Christmas Day, farmers with livestock still needed to tend to their animals. However, by bringing them off the hill this afternoon, he was making his job easier for the morrow.

I left the *vardo*, crossed the field and leaned on the gate to await Joe's arrival.

It fascinated me how, by hearing just a whistle or a short phrase, the dog responded to his master's instruction: twisting, turning, running left, or right, stopping and starting. The sheep, obviously in awe of the little animal, correspondingly moved to avoid it.

Apart from the odd veering off-line, they made their way down the track towards my gate. As they drew near, I called to the farmer.

"Shall I open the gate for you, Joe?"

"Yes, please, Romany, but step back when you do and make sure Raq is out of the way. They'll bunch together, and we don't want an accident."

I did his bidding, unlatching the heavy fastening and swinging back the wooden gate, which squealed on its metal hinges.

Sure enough, there was some jostling amongst the beasts as two, or three, abreast they passed through. They were now in the field in which the *vardo* rested.

"They'll not trouble you, Romany," said Joe, "but keep Raq on a rope when you're around them, just in case. As you can see, they're not overly fond of dogs."

I must say that I didn't feel either comforted or reassured by his last remark; however, I tried not to let my concern show. Instead, I turned the conversation to Christmas.

"You'll be all set for the big day, I suppose?"

"We are," he replied. "Sallie's cooking already; she's making enough mince pies to feed an army!"

"So what are your plans for tomorrow," I enquired.

"Up for milking, breakfast, down to the chapel, then lunch. I always likes to take a snooze after that, then back to milking."

"It's pretty well business as usual, then, Joe?"

"The beasts still have to be tended to; they don't look after themselves, you know," he smiled. "What's in store for you tomorrow?" he enquired.

"Well, I thought Raq and I would spend a cosy day in the *vardo*."

"You'd both be more than welcome at the house," Joe kindly offered, adding, "I know Sallie would love you to come over for lunch."

"If you're sure," I hesitatingly replied, whilst secretly having been hoping he might offer! The thought of cooking Christmas lunch on the fire had lost its appeal.

"Of course I'm sure. Would two o'clock suit you?"

I nodded, gratefully.

"See you tomorrow at two, then," he said, turning towards the farm. After a moment he stopped and turned about. "I think we might have a little snow overnight, Romany," he said.

"That would add a nice touch to the festive season," I responded.

"It might look nice," he said, "but it brings its difficulties to a farm. Let's hope it's just a sprinkling."

On arriving back at the *vardo*, a thought struck me. I had no gift to take to my kind friends at the farm. On opening the door and stepping inside, I saw the holly and ivy, and had a brainwave. I would make a Christmas wreath from some of it and give that to Sallie!

I took down some of my decoration and began weaving the garlands around a metal bucket, to form a circle, criss-crossing the foliage so as to lock it together. In no time at all I had a lovely wreath that Sallie could hang on her door. I temporarily hung it from the *vardo* door handle and stood back to admire my handiwork.

"She'll be pleased with that," I thought, and gave a little smile of pride in a job well done.

As the light began to fade, I noticed how cloudy and threatening the sky had become with a freshening breeze.

"Looks like Joe could be right," I said to Raq as I lit the lamps.

As I'd predicted, the *vardo* took on a golden glow. The heat from the lamps made it feel snug, and Raq soon settled down to sleep.

I was doing a little writing, when I was startled to hear Raq give a low growl.

"Someone's about," I thought, so, throwing back the outer door, I seized one of the lamps and held it aloft.

Imagine my surprise when I saw a dozen, or so, lanterns outside. A voice said, "One, two, three," and a choir of mixed adults' and children's voices began to sing the lovely carol, 'Away in a manger.'

Spellbound, I stood on the top step, as the clear voices rang across the fields.

When they had finished, I put down the lamp and applauded.

"Well done to you all. Step forward so that I can see you."

The group did as they were asked and I could see by the light of their lanterns that Arthur and his family were amongst the choristers.

"We were doin' the rounds of the local farms and Arthur reminded us that you were at Old Parks," said his father.

"I'm so glad you came," I told the assembly. "I've never had carols at my *vardo* door before."

"It's our pleasure, Romany," said another member.

"I know it's traditional to offer you mince pies," I told them, "but I haven't any, I'm afraid."

"This is our sixth farm," said Arthur's mother, "and I don't think I could eat another one, so don't worry."

"I could," Arthur chimed up, at which we all burst into laughter.

"We must be off. It's a long trek back to the village, and the weather's not looking good," another lady said.

"Merry Christmas to you all and thank you again for a lovely surprise," I called as they turned around and disappeared into the gloom. I watched their bobbing lanterns for a few minutes until the cold forced me back inside.

I lit the stove, as the *vardo* was now decidedly chilly. Leaving the door open had not been a good idea. However, once the fire had caught, the interior soon became comfortable again, and Raq dozed off once more.

I made ready my bed, extinguished the lamps, undressed in the dark and climbed in. Within a moment or two I was asleep and dreaming of Sallie's traditional Christmas lunch!

Chapter 10

A gift from above!

I awoke the following morning to an unusually bright *vardo*. Getting down from my bed, I drew aside a curtain and saw nothing but a blanket of white as far as my eye could see. Joe had been right, but we'd certainly had more than the sprinkling for which he had hoped.

I opened the *vardo* door to take a better look and suddenly Raq shot between my legs and jumped from the step, completely vanishing in the snow! I was shocked to see that a drift was almost level with the bottom of the door.

I hastily donned my trousers and ploughed into the snow, reaching down and finding Raq almost three feet beneath the surface. Placing my arms under his body, I hauled him out and carried him inside. Looking wet and bedraggled, the first thing he did was to shake himself vigorously, covering me and the *vardo* with wet snow. Now I was really cold and beginning to shiver.

Overnight the fire had gone out, so I put on some dry clothing and set-to lighting the fire.

After half an hour, I was feeling back to normal. I made some tea and fried some bacon on the stove. Thank goodness I had enough dry wood to last for a few days, or I'd freeze.

While having breakfast, my thoughts turned to the carollers.

"I hope they reached their homes before the snow started," I said to Raq.

Then another concern entered my head. I was due to visit Old Parks today. How would I fare crossing the field, when the snow was so deep? Raq couldn't possibly walk, as he'd sink; look what happened this morning. I'd have to carry him. Perhaps I should abandon the idea? Only my dreams of Sallie's lovely meal made the concept stay with me.

I passed half-an-hour staring wistfully out at the magical landscape. Although breezy, the sun was out, making the view look like a Christmas card illustration. What looked like a vast linen tablecloth was spread before me, and how beautiful it was that, as yet, it remained unmarred by footprints. Suddenly, the thought of footprints made me think of Joe's sheep. They should have been in my field. I went to each of the three windows, but there was simply no sign of them. I hadn't seen them from the doorway, either. That must mean that Joe had brought them in.

That idea relaxed me for a moment, but then I realised that the snow would have been disturbed, had Joe collected them. Where on earth might they be? Slowly the idea dawned that they might actually be buried somewhere in that sea of white. If it could happen to Raq, it could certainly have occurred with animals that had spent the night out-of-doors.

A cry of, "Romany, Romany," drifted into my consciousness. Opening the door, I could see Joe manfully wading towards the *vardo*, almost waist deep in snow. His arms were flailing from side-to-side, in an obvious effort to assist his passage.

"Everything's alright here, Joe," I called, "but where are your sheep?"

"I reckon they've sheltered behind a wall," he called. "Most probably they're covered by a drift. I'm looking for them now."

"Wait a moment and I'll help," I offered.

I hastily donned some warm clothing, a waterproof and windproof jacket, and my boots. Grabbing my stick, and leaving behind a sorrowful Raq, I closed the *vardo* door and descended into the deep snow.

Forcing my way through, I edged towards Joe. The snow rapidly found its way into my boots and my socks were soon sopping wet.

"Were do you suggest we begin, Joe?" I asked my friend.

"Well, the wind was blowing off the hill, so I reckon they'll have got into the lee of yonder wall to gain some shelter. Let's try there first."

Although a mere 100 yards distant, it was ten minutes before we were within touching distance of the wall. It felt as though we were wading through syrup, so resistant was the snow and I admit to having been a little breathless from the exertion.

The scale of the task was suddenly apparent. We were close to the gate where, the day before, I had watched Joe drive the animals through. The wall breasted the rise ahead of us and disappeared from sight. I looked at Joe and he nodded his head.

"I reckon I know what you're thinking, Romany. The wall's almost a mile long before it enters the next field, so that's how far we might have to go."

"It's a huge task, Joe, so the sooner we start, the better," I smiled, although I was inwardly daunted.

We began by Joe getting close-up to the wall and I positioned myself next to him. Then, as we advanced I used my stick to prod into the snow to my left, the idea being that we were sweeping the widest possible area, in case the sheep had not made it right up to the wall.

After only a few minutes, the awkwardness of the rolling gait I had to adopt, coupled with the effort required to push through the snow, were taking their toll. My breath was rasping; although physically quite fit, this was exercise at an extreme level.

We glanced at each other, and in an unspoken agreement stopped to catch our breath. I glanced back at the gate, and the reality that we'd not travelled very far, although it felt like miles, struck me.

"It's going to be dark before we reach the end, and there's no guarantee they're here," I puffed.

"I'd have brought the dog, but she'd not be able to make any headway in this soft stuff," Joe told me. "She'd be able to sniff them out," he ruefully added.

"I can see you're right, Joe, but what if we do find them? They won't be able to walk on this any more than the dog."

"We'll clear a space for them, and then I'll get some fodder over to them at some point. So long as they can move and breathe, they won't take any harm for one day."

Turning to face the task head, we began again that punishing routine. Imagine my delight when I felt my stick make contact with something that was obviously not the ground.

"I think I might have one," I said to Joe.

"Let's see," he breathlessly replied.

He too prodded with his stick, announcing, "I hope you're right."

Luckily he'd had the foresight, although I'm sure it was his farming experience, to bring a spade.

Gingerly, he dug down a foot, or so, exposing a woolly back, to our great relief.

He gave a whoop of delight. "We're on to them," he grinned.

He carefully cleared a space around the beast, which certainly seemed no worse for wear. Calmly, it looked up at us with those cold eyes, bent its head and purposefully chewed away at a small patch of flattened grass that Joe had exposed.

"If there's one here, then they're all here," Joe told me, adding, "Being sheep, they'll have all headed to the same spot."

Taking turns about with spade and sticks we slowly located and released fourteen animals, which Joe assured me was the size of his small flock.

"I'm more of a cattle farmer," he added.

"I'm so grateful that cattle were your preference," I laughed.

By the time the job was done, and I looked at my pocket watch, it was almost three o'clock!

When I gave Joe the time, he said, "Let's make tracks for the farm. T'missus'll be worrying about the dinner spoiling."

I indicated my wet clothing, and he told me that we'd go via the *vardo*, where I could collect some dry items, along with my patient dog.

Arriving back at the *vardo*, we were greeted by Raq's excited yelps. I gathered some dry clothing and placed them in my knapsack. There was no sense in putting them on, as they'd be just as wet as the set I was wearing by the time we ploughed our way to the farmhouse.

Taking Raq in his arms, Joe led the way, and I was happy to follow in his footsteps.

After what seemed an age, we stepped into the warm sanctuary of the kitchen. My nostrils were immediately assailed by the delicious smell of Christmas dinner. Their young son, Desmond, looked very relieved to see us. I think he was beginning to think he would never get any dinner! Sallie hugged me as we exchanged seasonal greetings.

"Take care, Sallie," I told her, "I'm soaked through."

"Eee, don't you fret, Romany. A bit o' wet never hurt anybody," she laughed, adding, "Now away and get changed before you catch pneumonia."

Her comment make me chuckle, as she seemed to contradict herself within the same sentence.

It would be boring of me to describe the veritable feast we enjoyed that late afternoon, but suffice to say that afterwards, I slumped in a comfortable chair by the fire and fell fast asleep, with Raq dozing by my side.

When I awoke, I took little persuading from Joe and Sallie to make my way upstairs and use one of their spare rooms for the night. I simply could not face that tortuous, wet trek back to the *vardo*.

Joe and Sallie Potter

Chapter 11

Spring at last!

Life was difficult on the farm as the snow lay deep right into the New Year but gradually the hard, and sometimes harsh, winter weather softened into Spring. The early snowdrops had graced the orchard and the slope down to the beck, a green tinge had hazed the trees and bushes as leaves began to appear, and, joy of joys, birdsong was beginning. The mornings were still sharp and crisp, but there was that unmistakable sense that Nature had woken up, and was ready for another explosion of joyous Life!

I had not been idle during the past couple of months. As well as my walks, often with Arthur, I had caught up with some writing, overhauled my hiding tent, sorted out various photographs, and lovingly prepared my fishing tackle in readiness for the opening of the trout season on the fifteenth of March. I had even finished a watercolour from the sketches I had made some while ago when I was a little farther North on the River Esk.

Despite the traumatic experience I had in North Yorkshire when the *vardo* was nearly washed away in a flood – as I described in my last book – I have a great love of water. Of course there is the lure of the trout, but more than that, water is the very 'life-blood' of our land. It has shaped our countryside, and it feeds it. Then there is the magical light that dances on the surface as the water flows……..and the sounds; tinkling streams, roaring falls, gurgling chuckles around boulders. In all this I fancy I hear the song of the water sprites!

Most of all, however, it is the wildlife of the water that I love to seek out. Arthur, I knew, particularly wanted to 'help' me photograph something, so I made my way through the trees down the sloping bank of the Daleraven Beck. I had in mind that we might watch the dippers which I believed to be nesting somewhere in the vicinity. I left Raq in the *vardo*, much to his disgust, although appreciative enough of the fatty lamb bone I left for him to gnaw. He loves dashing in and out of the beck, and on this occasion that would have entirely defeated my plan.

I settled down with my back to a tree and began my long reconnoitre. A robin twittered its plaintive little song from the branches above my head once he had decided I was no threat to him and he had ceased the irritated 'ticking' which he set up when I had first arrived.

Robin

Beyond I could hear the soft cooing of the woodpigeons, and, melting my heart, the haunting call of a curlew from the hills above where he has recently returned from his winter on the estuary. I will be off to find him before long – one of my favourite birds.

After an hour or so I moved cautiously a little farther along the beck-side. I had seen a dipper fly along once or twice, and heard the sharp and rapid "seet, seet, seet" call, and I gained the impression that activity was focussed on some tree roots which ran down into the water. Sure enough, after a few minutes in my new position I saw the birds going into a deep hollow in the bank underneath one of the roots. They were taking in bits of grass and moss to build their domed nest. It would not be possible to get to see the nest, being, as it was, in such an inaccessible location, but I knew what it would look like from an occasion when I had found a dippers' nest on a ledge underneath the arch of a bridge. I would have to describe it to Arthur as he wouldn't be able to see it for himself. However, with a bit of luck we *would* be able to watch the birds together.

Satisfied with my morning's observations I made my way back to the *vardo* to do a few jobs before Arthur came to see me after school later in the day.

"Hello, Romany," Arthur greeted me late in the afternoon. "I just heard a blackbird in the trees along yon' track. Seems like he was not sure of his song. He'd sing a little bit an' then repeat it. And then again, as if he were a practising."

I smiled and encouraged him to go on. "And what next, Arthur?"

"Why, he tried another short phrase, then he kept repeating that!" he replied.

"Excellent, Arthur. You have just described perfectly the song of the song thrush, a smaller cousin of the blackbird, but same family," I congratulated him. "I know that you recognise the song thrush by sight because we talked about him when we saw the redwings in the winter. Now you know his song."

"Right," said Arthur, rather puzzled. "With a name like *song* thrush I would have expected him to have a 'posher' song than the blackbird."

"Yes, Arthur, I see what you mean," I chuckled, "but there it is."

I then went on to tell him of my finding the dippers' nest site. "It's getting too dark to go and look today, but tomorrow is Saturday. Are you free, Arthur?"

"I have to do a few jobs on the farm in the morning, but I can be here by about midday, Romany," he replied, his eyes lit up in excitement.

"Then tomorrow afternoon it shall be!" I said. "Now, have you got time to share a bit of Sallie's cake?"

His eyes lit up still more, and we settled inside the *vardo* as the evening air was getting a little chilly.

The following day I had barely finished my bit of lunch when I saw an enthusiastic Arthur approaching.

"Are you ready, Romany?" he enquired eagerly.

"I am, Arthur, but before we go to the beck we need some materials," I explained.

Arthur looked puzzled so I told him of my plan to *build* a hide on the bank opposite the nest rather than use my hiding tent, which would be difficult to place on the slope between the trees.

I went to the back of the *vardo* where there is a cratch, or rack, where I keep all sorts of useful things, or things I *think* might be useful one day. I found a few straight sticks of reasonable length and handed them to Arthur. I then went inside the *vardo* for a ball of twine and I checked my jacket to make sure that my trusty pocket knife was there. We then set off across the field, through the trees, and down to the water's edge.

"We'll just put up the poles today," I said. "That way we shouldn't alarm the birds too much."

We found a good spot between two trees.

"We can use the trees themselves as our uprights, Arthur. We need to tie our poles together to make a sort of fence between them."

"What will we do then, Romany?" the boy asked.

"Find fallen branches, and vegetation to weave into our frame, but, as I said, not now. We need the birds to accept the frame first," I told him.

And so we set to and made the skeleton of our hide and then retired a little further away to watch for the dippers. Soon we saw them and were reassured that our engineering activities had not scared them.

"No nesting materials today, Arthur," I pointed out. "They must have finished building and now the hen will pop in from time to time to lay her eggs."

With his ever inquisitive mind Arthur asked, "How often will she lay, and how many eggs?"

"She'll lay an egg each day until the clutch is complete; probably four of five in all."

"So she'll be sittin' by next Saturday, Romany."

"Indeed, she should be," I replied.

I could see by the boy's face that he was going through a number of ideas in his mind following his calculation that the hen would be brooding her eggs by the following weekend. Then he asked, "And how long will she sit?"

"About two weeks, Arthur."

My answer was followed by more quizzical looks from the lad. Then he said, "So the hide really needs to be finished by next Saturday, otherwise we'll disturb her when she's sittin' won't we?"

"Yes, Arthur……but where is all this questioning leading?" I asked.

"Well, I really want to help build the hide, but until the evenings get lighter, I can only help at weekends. But then I don't want to delay the building of the hide either," he said pensively.

"I think the answer will lie in a compromise, Arthur," I said, smiling now that I knew what all his musings had been about.

"How do you mean," he rejoined.

"It is better if we don't do too much at any one time," I replied, "so, if I make a start putting up a bit of screening one or two days during the week, then by next Saturday, you will be able to help me finish the job. How does that sound?"

"Super," he agreed, reassured that the hide would be complete by the following weekend, but that he would still have a hand in it.

"I'd better be off now, Romany," he said. "Shall I see you tomorrow in chapel?"

"There'll be a bit of a problem if you don't, Arthur," I grinned. "They've invited me to take the service!"

"Till tomorrow then," he said, adding: "I'll go this way. Bye......and thanks."

So saying, he followed the beck a little way up-stream then climbed the steep slope through the trees towards the track home.

Chapter 12

We watch the Dippers

During the following week I made several trips to the beck-side, each time adding a little more vegetation to the hide. I was pleased to note that my activities did not seem to be upsetting the dippers. Even the ever vociferous robin was getting used to my presence for, although he still ticked me off, he did so rather less crossly, and he soon stopped and reverted to his melancholy warble.

I had also spent a very pleasant day on the Fells. Old Parks itself is pretty high and hilly; beautiful rounded grassy hills, many graced with magnificent oaks, such as the view I see from where my *vardo* is now *atched* (the *Romani* word for 'stopped'). I can think of no better spot to have my ashes scattered when my time comes.

To the West the great hills of the Lake District can be seen, but, as I said before, I am fonder of the massive Fells to be seen to the East, king among them being the awesome Cross Fell. My walk this time, however, had been to nearer Fells just beyond the neighbouring village of Gamblesby.

As I have mentioned before, I love the call of the curlew, and as I climbed to the higher ground I was treated not only to their "coo-lee, coo-lee" calls, but also to the tremulous and bubbling song – I think my favourite of all sounds.

When Saturday came, Arthur arrived while I was still washing up my breakfast things.

"Not too early am I, Romany," he asked.

"Gosh no, Arthur, I've been up for ages, but I decided to go for a walk before having breakfast" I assured him.

"See anything interesting?" enquired the boy.

"I did indeed," I said, then added, "But I always do, for Nature is never dull if you look hard enough for her little secrets and miracles."

Arthur thought about this for a while then said, "Did you see anything *exciting*, then?"

I smiled at the way he had responded to my deliberately provocative answer to his former question.

"I rather think you would have enjoyed the buzzard I saw being worried by a raven," I said.

"Isn't the buzzard able to make short work of a raven? With his sharp beak and claws, I mean," Arthur queried.

I then explained to him that although the buzzard does certainly have a formidable hooked bill, and large strong talons, for some reason, when he is mobbed or worried by other birds, even those much smaller than himself, he seldom shows any sign of retaliating, but simply slips and slides deftly out of the way of any attacks, eventually soaring away to a more peaceful location, often at a great height. And he achieves all this by just tilting his huge outstretched wings. He hardly ever flaps his wings to avoid his assailants.

"But going back to your question, Arthur," I continued, "I would say that the raven would actually be quite a match for the buzzard. He's pretty well the same size if not a fraction larger – a point you realise when you see them close together – and he has an awesome looking dagger of a bill. He is also an aerial expert in his own right. I wouldn't like to give odds on who would win in a *real* conflict, but the truth is, these skirmishes are seldom, if ever, serious fights. It's all about making a point, and that point is usually, 'I don't want you on my patch!' "

I had by this time put everything away in the *vardo*, so, calling Raq to heel, we set off for Daleraven Beck. We made our way down towards the water keeping in line with the almost completed hide.

"Why, it's all finished, Romany," exclaimed Arthur betraying some disappointment.

"No it isn't, Arthur," I replied. We still have a roof to put on."

"Why do we need a roof?" he asked.

"So that any bird flying over us won't see us and give the alarm to the dippers," I explained. Blackbirds in particular will let off an explosion of an alarm call if he spots us sitting in here."

Arthur, pleased that he would, after all, be helping to finish the hide took my all-purpose pocket knife and cut some well leafed boughs to weave into the framework of the roof. Meanwhile I had dragged across a long log I had spotted so that we could use it as a seat. After half an hour or so I felt the hide was pretty well as ready as it needed to be.

"Just one thing left, Arthur. Can you think what that is?" I asked.

"Well, I guess we need to do something about a window otherwise we won't be able to see the birds," he replied shrewdly.

"Absolutely right. We each need to sit here on the log and then make a gap in the foliage just large enough to get a view of the beck," and so saying I carefully formed my own spy hole. Arthur did the same.

I suggested that we then leave the scene for the birds to settle down again after our roof-building activities, promising that we would return in the afternoon to do our first bit of dipper watching.

Back at the *vardo* I had little difficulty in persuading Arthur to share some bread and bacon – a typical Gypsy meal. As we sat and munched away swallows, freshly back from Africa and just starting to nest in the farm buildings, wheeled around overhead searching for their own lunch – as many flies as they could catch. A beautiful sight, but I preferred my food to theirs!

In the distance the buzzard gave its mewing call, the incident with the raven long forgotten. Then the sound of the curlews came down on the breeze, and I felt very contented.

"You're smiling to yourself, Romany," remarked Arthur.

"Just enjoying the wonderful sights and sounds of Nature," I replied. Arthur nodded and smiled too.

In the afternoon we made our way down to the hide. For once the robin didn't start up his 'ticking,' or maybe he just wasn't there to see us, so we were able to creep into our hide undetected by the dippers. We had taken the precaution of bringing some old sacks to sit on as the log was rather hard, and also a bit damp. These makeshift cushions greatly improved our comfort.

We carefully peeped out to survey the scene before us. As luck would have it one of the dippers was standing on a rock in the beck. It curtseyed and bobbed endlessly.

"He looks like he's got ants in his pants," whispered Arthur.

"Yes, he doesn't stay still much does he?" I agreed. "He does it for camouflage," I explained quietly. "If you look at the moving water and notice the way the light dances and flickers on the ever-moving water-mirror, you will see that the dipper is actually blending in quite well, his white breast like a patch of light on the water constantly dancing."

Just then the dipper jumped off his boulder and disappeared into the water. Arthur looked most concerned, but I explained that the dipper feeds under water and would come to no harm. A moment later the bird emerged from the water using its wings to help propel itself out of the water and back onto the rock. It had a couple of juicy larvae in its bill, and after a few quick curtseys it flew with rapid wing beats into the hollow where we had deduced the nest was located under the tree roots.

"As I thought, Arthur," I said. "That must be the male bird we've been watching, and the female must be sitting on the eggs. He's taking food to her."

"Couldn't you tell whether it was male or female by the colours?" asked Arthur.

"No. The birds both have the same plumage." I replied.

"Look; he's out again!" said Arthur as the dipper reappeared and sped off down-stream.

We had a little time to wait before the dipper returned. In a flash he was suddenly dancing on his favourite rock again, another meal for his lady in his bill. After feeding her this time the male stayed around flitting from one boulder to another, but always bobbing up and down each time he perched.

The Dipper blinking

As we watched he walked down the sloping edge of the rock and continued walking right into the water until he was completely submerged and out of our sight.

"It makes me think back to your sermon last Sunday, Romany," giggled Arthur. I looked mystified.

"You told us about Jesus waking on the water and Peter trying to do the same but sinking, but Jesus told him to have faith," he reminded me.

"Yes, I did. Quite right, Arthur," I replied.

"Well, yon bird is walking *in* the water instead of on it, but it still seems like a miracle to me," came back the boy.

I then told him how it was the dipper's usual method of searching for food and that in reasonably placid water he could grip the bottom with his feet and defy the natural buoyancy which was always trying to send him back to the surface, but in rougher water he needs to use his wings to help propel him along.

The dipper then emerged from the depths with yet another larva. After a few curtseys he took his prize into his hidden mate.

"Next time he stands on that rock bobbing, Arthur, I want you to watch him very closely," I told him. "Pay particular attention to the eyes."

Arthur duly studied our dancing dipper next time he settled on the rock. Then he said with great excitement, "His eyes keep turning white, Romany!"

"Well spotted," I commended him. "Actually, he has white eyelids and as he 'dips' he blinks."

I then told him that I wanted him to discover one more thing about our dipper, and this time to use his ears. It was not an easy task for him with the constant gurgling of the water, but after a while his face lit up and I knew that he had heard what I too had just heard.

"He made a sort of stuttering whistle. I'm sure he did!" said Arthur.

"Right again. Well done!" I said. "That 'zweety, zweet, zweet' is what passes for his song. Not impressive as song birds go, but more tuneful than the call he makes as he flies along the beck."

After watching our dipper feed his wife a few more times we quietly left the hide and made our way back to the *vardo*. Having been away from his family all day I thought it right not to invite Arthur to stay for supper, so in the late afternoon I suggested he might like to go and tell his family what he had learned about dippers.

"But, before you go you can practice on me," I suggested, "starting with a description."

"When we first saw them I thought they were black and white birds," Arthur began, "but watching them more closely I've seen that the black is really a dark brown, and the tummy is chestnut coloured."

"Good, Arthur. You're spot on. What about size and shape?" I asked.

"Fattish, like a puffed up robin," he replied, "and somewhere between a robin and a blackbird in size, but dumpier than a blackbird."

Arthur then went on to recall the curtseying for camouflage, the blinking eye, the walking under water – assisted by the wings when needed, and he even made a pretty good imitation of its call and its song.

"Excellent, Arthur," I congratulated him. "I think you are destined to be a true naturalist!"

He went off a happy lad.

Chapter 13

The Fells

One afternoon the following week I was sitting by the *vardo* when I thought I caught the sound of singing. I stood up and saw a familiar figure strolling up the track which comes across the fields from Kirkoswald. It was Arthur, and as he got closer he spotted me and quickened his pace, his serenade at an end. I was not surprised that he had been singing as I knew he had a good voice and sang up well in the chapel. In fact, in years to come, Arthur was destined to be a key member of the Glassonby Singers.

"Hello, Romany," he greeted me.

"What brings you this way?" I asked in reply.

"I usually go to school on my bike," Arthur explained, "but I've got a puncture. Dad took me in this morning in his trap, but I've just walked home, and this is quicker than by road."

"But not suitable for your bicycle," I said, understanding the situation, "which is why I don't normally see you on this track."

"No, it would shake my bike to bits," he agreed.

"And it wouldn't be very comfortable for you, either," I grinned.

Arthur set down his satchel and sat down on the grass beside me.

"As it's not dark yet can we go and have another look at the dippers?" he asked.

"I don't see why not," I replied, and I called Raq from a distant slope where he had been chasing rabbits. I think it's just a game to him, for he knows by now that he will never catch one! To his disgust, I shut the dog in the *vardo* and we made our way through the orchard and down to the hide.

Under the trees it was more apparent that the afternoon light was failing, but we could see well enough to get some more good views of the dipper, still regularly feeding his sitting mate.

We didn't stay too long as Arthur wanted to be home before it was fully dark, but, once again the hide had served us well. Arthur bade me farewell, and set off.

"Your bicycle has given me an idea," I called after him. He stopped and tuned, waiting to see if I would explain.

"When you've repaired your puncture we can go to the Fells," I said.

"But you haven't got a bike, Romany," he called back.

"No, Arthur, but I've got Comma," and I put up my hand in a final wave. I would expand on the plan I was hatching at a later date. He took the hint and set off again.

The next day there was no Arthur coming along the track in the afternoon so I concluded that the bicycle was in operation once more. That evening I walked down to Midtown Farm and checked with Arthur's parents that it would be all right to take Arthur up onto the Fells. They were quite happy about the idea so early the following Saturday I went down to the Kidd's farm again, this time on Comma's warm back. Arthur was ready and waiting in the yard by his bicycle.

Arthur with his bicycle

Raq, who had been trotting along beside Comma, gave a bark of delight on seeing the farm collie, and the two dogs began a friendly game of chase and romp.

Armed with a generous packed lunch which Arthur's mother had provided for us – it was a good job there wasn't too much else in my rucksack – we set off, Arthur on his cycle, I on Comma, and Raq running around us in excitement, sensing that an adventure was afoot.

A mile or two along the lane, Arthur cycled up alongside Comma and grinned up at me.

"What is it, Arthur?" I asked.

"I was just remembering last winter," he replied. "I was up here then and I heard a reet concert."

"Go on," I encouraged him, intrigued to hear more.

"Well, it was the Cowperthwaite brothers, Robin and Joss. They were ploughing alongside each other singing duets at the tops of their voices," he explained.

"Were they good?" I asked, chuckling.

"O yes; very good," said the boy. He then pointed and said, "That's one of our fields."

"What, right over here, Arthur, how come?" I asked.

"Most of the farms hereabouts seem to have a field or two across here. It's known as Farlands," he told me.

"Is that why it's *called* Farlands – because the fields are far away from the farms to which they belong?" I queried.

"Not sure, Romany, but it seems likely," and he dropped back to following Comma.

We entered the village of Gamblesby, turned right, and made our way to Tarnside Farm. Opposite the farmhouse a man was sitting sketching the little church. As we approached I recognised him as the local Minister, the Reverend Sinclair Walker. I dismounted and walked across to talk to him, and to look at his drawing.

"Very nice, Sinclair," I congratulated him.

"And what brings you here?" he asked smiling.

"I'm just going to leave my mare, Comma, at Tarnside Farm, then young Arthur here and I will be off to the Fells for the day," I enlightened him.

St. John's ~ Gamblesby.

Rev Sinclair Walker's drawing of St John's Gamblesby

After a few more pleasantries, I took Comma into the farm, greeting Mr Pattinson who had previously agreed to stable her for the day.

"You've made it then," he greeted me.

"I have indeed, Tom," I replied.

At that point his wife Margaret and their son Thomas, who I had seen at Kirkoswald School, came out to see what was happening. When I had explained about my intended day on the Fells, the look in Thomas's eyes told their own story.

"Do you think young Thomas would like to come with us?" I asked; "We've more than enough food for three."

"O yes, please, please," cried Thomas, looking at his parents in eager anticipation.

And so it was that the three of us and Raq set off up the little lane just beyond the church and made our way towards the Fells. As we walked I pointed out the various birds we saw. These included blackbirds, chaffinches, a robin, a couple of greenfinches, and, overhead, crows and jackdaws. In a distant field we could see lapwings.

Lapwing

Between these sightings, Thomas explained why his father's farm was called Tarnside when there is no sign of any water. Apparently, there had been a little tarn or pond, but when it was decided to build a church for the village the site of the tarn was selected, and so it was filled in and the church built on the spot. A bit ambitious maybe, but then Winchester Cathedral was built on a swamp, and that has stood the test of time, albeit with a little underpinning!

We crossed the road down from Hartside and climbed up onto Melmerby Fells, following the line of a dry-stone wall. On this wall a dainty little black and white bird alighted and flicked its tail. I halted the boys and told them to keep still and watch. Deciding we were no threat it dropped down and disappeared into a hole in the wall.

"Let's sit here for a while and watch," I suggested, and I got my binoculars ready for Arthur and Thomas to use.

"It was a pied wagtail. Look, there he goes," I said as the bird flew off again. "That will be the male feeding his sitting mate," I explained, "unless the eggs have hatched, in which case both parents will be feeding the nestlings." As we sat and watched, the frequency of visits with food made it clear that it was, indeed, both parents feeding the young.

We continued on our way, and where the stone wall veered off to the right we continued straight on, uphill, following a sheep track. Suddenly our attention was caught by something that flew, somewhat noisily, past us and dropped down into the ling beyond us.

"Gosh," said Thomas. "That must have been

Pied wagtail

that smallest bird you were telling us about at school."

I smiled and replied, "That small bird was actually a large dragonfly. I'm pretty certain I know which type, but let's try to find it to be sure."

We set off cautiously, keeping our eyes fixed on the heather. The dragonfly obligingly flew up and resettled pin-pointing for us its whereabouts. I had a quick glance through the binoculars then handed them to the boys to have a look.

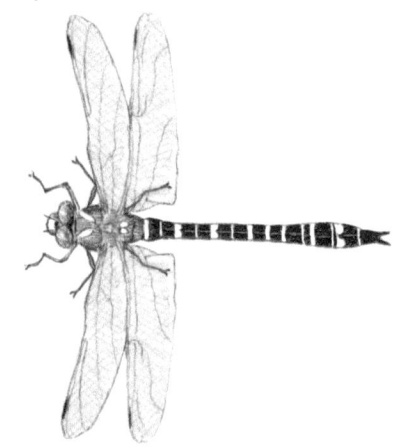

Goldenring dragonfly

"Wow," said Arthur. "It's like an enormously long wasp!"

"Long black body," I confirmed, "with distinct yellow bands. It also has huge emerald green eyes."

We managed to get a little closer before it flew off to hunt in another area.

"What does it eat, Romany?" enquired Thomas

89

"O, insects mainly. Dragon-flies are voracious creatures and some species will even eat other, dragonflies and damsel flies," I replied.

"Nice," murmured Arthur, wrinkling up his nose.

"It is well named," I pointed out, "for it's a goldenring dragonfly."

The next thing of interest we discovered was a merlin. I had spotted it in the distance as it flew low over the horizon. I asked the boys if they were up for a bit of crawling to get to a bit of rough vegetation ahead which might give us sufficient cover to watch out for the merlin, for I guessed it would be nesting in the area and therefore, likely to return. Accordingly, we edged our way forward and crept into the cover of some dense broom.

By mutual consent we decided it was time to have our lunch, so, while we waited for the merlins we enjoyed our thickly cut, generously filled sandwiches and some of Isabella Kidd's wonderful fruit cake.

"We'll have to wait a bit for our drink, I'm afraid," I told the boys. "I know of a nice clear beck, but I don't want us to move just yet. Let's just wait a little longer to see if the merlins will appear again."

Shortly after that we had the great good fortune to see this small falcon come into sight and settle on a rock ahead of us.

In its talons it had what seemed to be a meadow pipit. After a brief pause it flew down into the ling and was lost from sight. A minute or two later it flew off to hunt again.

"Probably feeding the hen bird," I said.

Male Merlin

"Why, does it nest on the ground?" enquired Arthur.

"It does indeed. But I think it would be unkind for all three of us to go and look for it. I would hate to be responsible for making her desert."

I decided it was time to begin our return walk so we headed back, keeping to the right of the track we had been following so that we would take in some more of the Fells. I was thrilled to be able to point out the curlews for Arthur and Thomas, and to get them to listen to and enjoy their bubbling song. Yes, I will say it again – my favourite sound!

So it was, after a most enjoyable day on my beloved Fells we arrived back at Gamblesby through the top end of the village, passing Hilltop Farm, the hill being the location from which John Wesley, the famous preacher who founded the Methodist movement, had once preached.

"Hello Edwin," I called as we passed Brookside Farm, the home of the Toppin family.

"Hello. Nice to see you," he replied.

"All well with you, I asked.

"Aye," he replied. "You know we have another new bairn – little Edith."

"I didn't. Congratulations," I said, and we continued on down through the village back to Tarnside, where we collected Comma and bade farewell to Thomas.

"Well, Raq, old man," I said to the dog," you've been on such good behaviour today, I shall find a special treat for you when we get home.

And by the time we did get home it was dark. As we approached Midtown Farm the lights from the windows looked most welcoming.

"Look at all the moths fluttering against the kitchen window," I said to Arthur. "In fact, seeing moths reminds me of a bird I've heard is to be seen on Lazonby Fell ….. but I'll tell you about that another time.

Chapter 14

We photograph the foxes

The following day I felt the lure of the river. During the day I checked through my fishing tackle, taking particular care to ensure that my fly line was well greased. I also tied a couple of very bushy flies, for my quarry was to be the elusive sea trout. Fishing for them is best done after dark, and a bushy fly causes a wake on the surface of the water which sea trout seem to find irresistible. Unfortunately, nine times out of ten they just dash at the fly, give it a sharp tug, and swim away, their curiosity satisfied, or maybe happy that they have scared off an intruder into their territory. But sometimes one strikes lucky, and the fish is hooked.

It was, therefore, with eager anticipation that I set off with Raq just before dusk to follow the beck down to Daleraven Bridge and beyond to the banks of the River Eden. I found a suitable spot to ask Raq to stay and 'guard' my shoes and socks which I sat and took off. I then rolled up my trousers and waded into the chilly water.

In the distance I heard the sharp bark of a dog fox, answered by the eerie screech of a vixen even further off. I knew this would have Raq's hackles rising so I softly called to reassure him. This reminded me that I had promised Arthur that we would go to watch the foxes in the quarry. By now it was likely that the fox cubs would be old enough to venture out. I was so busy musing on the foxes that I was not prepared when a sharp tug came on my line. I was too late to strike; the terms we anglers use to describe pulling back sharply to try to hook the fish.

"That's one of my chances missed," I murmured to myself as I cast my line out across the river again.

In fact, I missed several more times as sea trout tantalised me by tugging fiercely at my fly and then spitting it out before I had the chance to strike. But no matter: it was a beautiful night. A water vole plopped into the water behind me, a tawny owl hooted waveringly in the trees beyond, and the ghostly shape of a barn owl floated silently along following the line of the opposite bank. No wonder I kept losing concentration on my fishing.

Suddenly, there was a mighty tug. I swiftly lifted my rod tip high and became very excited as I felt the thuds of a sizeable sea trout securely hooked at the end of my line. That was merely the start, of course, I now had to 'play' and land the fish ...... and there's many a slip, as it is so truly said!

Raq clearly sensed what was happening for he gave a bark and excited whimper.

"*Kushto jukal*," I called;' "Stay."

With great power the fish swam rapidly upstream, my reel screaming as he took more line. Then the moment all anglers dread – nothing. The line went slack. I knew the fish was now racing back downstream to-wards me, and all the time the line is slack, the fish has a greater chance of slipping the hook. I stripped the

Sea Trout

line back as fast as I could, letting it drop in the water at my feet for there was no time to *reel* the line back. At last I had the fish tight again, and from then on I played the fish with the fly line held between fingers and thumb, the reel redundant. At last the fish tired – and I admit I did too – and I netted a gleaming silver sea trout of some four or five pounds.

After that I sat on the bank for a while beside Raq, simply enjoying the beauty of the night. The moon, now fully up produced myriad dancing lights on the ever flowing water, a bat dipped over the surface, the breeze rustled the leaves, and a mixture of those heady riverside smells tickled my nostrils.

"This is the life," I said to the dog. Raq looked up at me, the moonlight in his large dark eyes. I swear he understood. Eventually I put my shoes and socks back on, lit my storm lamp and began the walk back to the *vardo*.

During the next few days I visited the quarry to look for the foxes and to see where Arthur and I might secret ourselves to watch them. I was delighted to find that there was semi-circle of shrubbery which would be an ideal spot to conceal ourselves without the need for the hiding tent I had been expecting to have to use.

The next time Arthur came to see me at the *vardo* I said, "When you have a day free, Arthur, we'll go to the quarry to try to get a photograph of the fox cubs.

"Super," he replied. "Are you sure they'll be there?"

"O, I think so," I replied, but I didn't want to let him know that I had already checked it out in case he felt disappointed that I hadn't taken him with me for my reconnoitre.

"As it happens," said Arthur, "I'm free tomorrow."

"Then tomorrow it shall be," I said.

"Just enough light left for another visit to the dippers, isn't there, Romany?" asked the lad, as he often did when he called to see me after school.

My smile was my answer, and we made our way down to our hide, the leaves of which were now dried and withered, but it still did its job. After a short while we became aware that there were rather more than two dippers, and some of them were much less striking in their plumage.

"Those are the young ones, now fledged and out with their parents, learning how to find food," I explained, "but they're still pretty reliant on their parents for food."

To illustrate the point, a parent bird settled beside one of its offspring, both curtseying, and gave it a nice fresh morsel.

"I'm glad you've seen that, Arthur," I said, "it's always nice when we've been watching a pair of nesting birds to see the youngsters safely fledged."

"Will they stay here, Romany?" asked Arthur.

"They will remain on this stretch of the beck, but not now necessarily at this particular spot. I suspect our hide has now served its purpose," I replied.

"Goodbye, dippers," said Arthur philosophically as we departed, "we've enjoyed your company!"

The following morning we set off for the quarry. I left Raq behind as I knew he would find the close proximity of foxes too tempting to keep completely quiet, and, more importantly, I didn't want the foxes to catch Raq's scent. It would be hard enough trying to keep our own scent down wind of the wily foxes.

To that end, I tested the wind direction so as to plan the best way to approach the quarry – it's always best to approach a wild animal with the wind on your face; that way your scent is carried away from the creature. We cautiously made our way into the cover of the bushes and settled down to wait. I set up my camera on its tripod, which had been very heavy to carry, so that the camera was above the top of the bushes, and was focused on the clearing where I had previously seen the fox cubs playing. We ourselves kept low down, peeping through the greenery. I had a remote release cable for the camera, and I gave it to Arthur to hold.

"Squeeze the end firmly when I give the word, Arthur," I said, "but we may have to wait a while."

"I'm not going anywhere in a hurry," he grinned, and we began our wait.

"What's that scratchy song?" asked Arthur.

"A whitethroat," I replied, and turning round I pointed it out to him. It was perched on the top of a nearby bush, its throat puffed out as he pushed out his song.

"He's a member of the warbler family," I added.

Arthur then nudged me excitedly. I turned back and there, in the sunlit clearing were three fox cubs, rolling, chasing each other, and generally enjoying a rough and tumble.

Whitethroat

"Hold steady, Arthur. We'll wait to see if they'll keep just a little more still before we try a photograph," I said.

At that moment, as if by magic they all sat on their haunches looking in the same direction.

"Now," I whispered, and I heard the camera shutter click as Arthur promptly responded to my command.

Three young foxes

The reason why the foxes had stopped their game then became apparent. The vixen appeared with a young rabbit in her jaws. The fox cubs made excited high pitched whimpering sounds and dropped their heads, ready to feed on the prize their mother was bringing. She dropped the rabbit in front of them and pandemonium broke out as the cubs jostled for a chance to tear off a tasty joint.

Swallowing a tiny fly, I involuntarily let out a cough, and in an instant the foxes had gone, but not before one of them, I couldn't see which, had grabbed the remains of the rabbit.

"I think that will be it for today," I said to Arthur, "I'm so sorry."

"Don't apologise," replied Arthur, "that was fantastic. I've seen foxes crossing the fields in the distance before, but nothing like this." He then added, "Do you think the photo will be any good?"

"I'm sure it will be," I assured him. "I could hear the camera shutter at exactly the right time."

We made our way back to the *vardo* pleased with our expedition. That evening, using the temporary dark room Joe had allowed me to set up in one of the out-houses at the farm, I developed the photograph. It was a great success, and the following day I gave it to a very proud Arthur to take home and show his parents, his brother Norman, and his sister Margaret.

Chapter 15

We take to the road

To avoid the possibility of disappointing Arthur I went to see his parents one day when I knew Arthur would be at school. I had been hatching a plan ever since the night we returned from the Fells and watched the moths at the lighted kitchen window at Midtown Farm. I explained my plan over a cup of tea and a generous helping of plate cake.

"It's okay with us," John Kidd said, "but are you sure it won't be any trouble to you?"

"Arthur will be no bother at all," I said, "I'll enjoy the company. So it's all right for me to ask him?"

"Definitely," replied his mother.

When I next saw Arthur I asked him if he remembered what I had said about a bird I believed to be at Lazonby Fell.

"I do remember, Romany," he answered, "but you didn't actually say what it was."

"You're right, Arthur, I didn't," I agreed. I wanted to formulate a plan before saying more."

"And now you have?" he enquired.

"Yes, Arthur, I have," and I went on to tell him that the bird was a nightjar, and that its main source of food is moths.

Arthur nodded as he recollected that it had been my seeing moths that had caused me to mention the bird.

"The problem I've had to sort out is two fold, Arthur," I continued. "Firstly the nightjar is pretty inactive during the daytime, and secondly, Lazonby Fell is a good deal farther away then Melmerby Fell.

Arthur started to look a bit downcast, as if this was going to be one of those nice ideas that just wouldn't work out.

"So, Arthur," I went on, "we would need to stay overnight at Lazonby Fell. I've had a word with your parents, and they are very happy for you to come with me for a couple of days away in the *vardo*. I know you are on holiday from school next week, so we can do it soon."

Arthur looked so excited that I thought he might burst. For a while he didn't seem able to speak. He just grinned from ear to ear.

"Really? Honestly, Romany?" he burst out at last.

"Yes, really. Yes, honestly," I assured him smiling at his obvious pleasure. We then got down to the serious business of planning our expedition.

A few days later we packed the *vardo* steps inside the waggon and backed Comma into the shafts. She seemed pleased to be back in harness, and Raq ran round excitedly knowing that an adventure was afoot.

The *vardo* creaked, as it always did, as Comma took the strain. She pulled the *vardo* around and back onto the track leading back through the farmyard.

Sallie came to the door to wave us off as we passed the farmhouse, young Desmond at her side. Joe was, by now, out on the farm somewhere.

"Safe journey!" she called.

"Thanks," I replied. "See you in a few days."

We made our way through Glassonby – we did not stop at Midtown Farm as Arthur had said goodbye to his family before coming up to Old Parks to join me at the *vardo*. We took the road to Kirkoswald where I pulled off so that we could walk into the town to buy some provisions; not that we needed much after we had been plied with goodies by both Sallie and Arthur's mother, Isabella!

From Kirkoswald we took the road to Lazonby which we entered soon after passing over the Eden Bridge where, as the road was quiet, I couldn't resist halting Comma and putting on the brake so that I could look over the parapet of the bridge down into the steadily flowing waters of the Eden. Arthur stood beside me and we took in the scene together in silence. That pleased me. An instinctive feel for the moments when words are superfluous, even unwelcome, is a rare gift and I was pleased Arthur possessed it.

We climbed back onto the footboard, made our way through Lazonby and headed out on the Heskett road. As soon as we had cleared the village I pulled off onto a wide verge so that we could have some lunch.

"I was ready for this, Romany," said Arthur, tucking into a massive ham sandwich.

"Me too," I agreed, "and Comma is enjoying that lush grass." She had her head down munching contentedly, watched by Raq who had also been given some 'lunch.'

As we sat eating, a small brown bird alighted on a nearby post. Arthur looked at me questioningly.

"Spotted flycatcher," I told him.

"Ah – he's gone," said Arthur as the bird dashed into the air.

"Maybe not," I replied. "Watch."

The flycatcher re-turned to the post almost before I had finished speaking.

"How did you know that?" asked the boy' "Have you got second sight?"

"A lot of people think that Gypsies do have second sight, Arthur, but, no, it's nothing so grand; I just know the typical behaviour of the spotted flycatcher. Once he's found a suitable perch he sits

Spotted flycatcher

there until an insect flies by, then he dashes off to catch it, returns to his perch and waits for the next one."

We made do with a cold drink to save lighting the stove or making a fire whilst still journeying, then we continued our journey through the woodland and up to Lazonby Fell. By late afternoon we reached a suitable place to stop, or *atch*. I released Comma to graze, securing her in the Romani manner using a plug chain.

"Before we prepare our supper, let's use the daylight to explore the area, Arthur," I said, and calling Raq to heel we set off.

Lazonby Fell is much less rugged, and also less high, than the Fells of the Pennines, more like heath-land, and with many trees. I saw at once how ideal this habitat would be for the nightjar.

"What we need to look out for, Arthur, is a clearing with a post or dead tree in or near it. The nightjar can't resist such perches," I explained.

"Like that," said Arthur turning to his left and pointing to the ideal spot.

"Yes, Arthur, well done!" I praised him, "and we have these trees behind us to give us some cover until it's fully dark. Perfect."

We returned to the *vardo*, collected some wood for a fire and got down to the serious business of supper. When we had finished Raq licked the plates while I asked Arthur to show me his handkerchief. He looked perplexed but dutifully held up a brown check specimen.

"I'll get you another one," I said, mystifying him even more, and after rummaging through my clothes locker I presented him with a white handkerchief.

"Put that in your pocket, Arthur. I'll explain why you need it when the time comes," I told him.

We re-traced our steps to the clearing, aiming to arrive there just as dusk was fading into night. Positioning ourselves near some trees so that the moonlight would not make us too obvious we began our vigil. We'd not long to wait before a low but persistent 'churring' sound started – less harsh than a cricket but more sustained. It went on for about ten seconds and then shifted up a semi-tone for a while, and then returned to its original note – all without a break. This alternation kept on for some minutes.

"That's the song of the nightjar," I whispered to Arthur.

Another bird then began to 'churr', farther away, and instead of going up in pitch this one dropped to a lower and quieter note, but, like the first nightjar, it kept up these alternating 'churrings' for minutes on end.

"Keep your eyes on that dead branch", I said. "Hopefully one of the nightjars will come to perch there, then we should get a pretty good view. With this amount of moonlight we should be able to use the binoculars."

Just then an unearthly squeal cut through the night air causing Arthur to jump.

"What was *that*?" asked the boy.

"I think that was probably a rabbit being taken by a stoat or weasel," I said.

"How can a little thing like a weasel cope with something as large as a rabbit?" enquired Arthur.

"It will stalk its way stealthily nearer and nearer to the rabbit, and then, when close enough, leap up and sink its teeth into the rabbit's neck," I explained. "I have even seen the little creature then drag his prize off to his nest."

"Look, Romany," said Arthur in an excited whisper.

I followed his gaze and saw a nightjar perched, as I had hoped, on the dead branch. It immediately began its 'churring' song for us. That started off another nightjar. After a while the more distant bird flew into sight and flapped around showing white patches on its wings and tail.

"You see those white patches, Arthur?" I whispered; "that's why we've brought our white hankies."

Arthur still looked puzzled.

"But I don't want to use them yet," I continued, "while we can still watch this perched bird."

A short while after the second bird appeared, however, the perched nightjar flew up, making toward the flying bird. There was a series of loud 'cracks' from the air and some sharp calls as both birds disappeared from sight.

"That sound was the nightjar clapping his wings, Arthur," I told him, "and that 'kweet, kweet' call, like the clapping, was to warn off the intruder from his territory."

Nightjars

All was then quiet for a while so I said to Arthur, "now it's our turn to pretend we are intruding nightjars. With a bit of luck we'll get our nightjar to fly really close to us."

I explained that the white handkerchief, when flapped aloft, will make the nightjar think it's the white patches on another male nightjar's wings and tail, and clapping our hands smartly every few seconds will sound like a nightjar clapping its wings. I suggested that Arthur should flap the hankie and I clap my hands.

"Okay," said Arthur, giggling at the spectacle we made. However, his eyes opened wide in amazement and pleasure when our ruse worked and our nightjar appeared again, as if by magic, and swooped around just over us, affording us magnificent views.

Eventually, deciding either that we were, in fact, no threat, or, perhaps, that we were too formidable intruders to cope with, the bird disappeared again. We took that as our cue to make our way back to the *vardo*. On the way back I picked up the carcase of a rabbit. It was fresh and in good condition. The teeth marks confirmed my suspicion that it was the rabbit we had heard squeal earlier. I slung it over my shoulder.

The following day I suggested that we might go to look for the nightjars' nest. Arthur was, of course, all for the idea, although I did warn him that the chances of success were but slim.

"Bacon and eggs have never tasted so good, Romany," said Arthur as we set off after breakfast and made our way back to the clearing.

"That's the fresh air and the adventure, my boy," I replied smiling; "but if truth be told, your mother's breakfasts are much better, but perhaps less exciting!"

At the scene of last night's happenings, I stood and took stock.

"The male was serenading from that tree there," I mused aloud, "so his mate will be within a reasonable distance of that."

"Where do nightjars nest?" asked Arthur.

"On the ground, where their mottled plumage makes an exceptionally good camouflage," I replied, "and that area of bracken over there on the edge of the clearing and near to the trees would be a likely spot ... or maybe that bracken over there," and I pointed to a similar site on the other side of the clearing.

We made our way to the first area of bracken and began cautiously moving through the fronds.

"Do keep your eyes ahead of your feet, Arthur," I told him. "Nightjars blend in so well with the fallen dead bracken and the shadows of the new growth it is all too easy to tread on a sitting bird."

We searched for an hour or more. We found a willow warbler's nest but no nightjars.

"Let's turn our attention to the other patch of bracken," I said when I felt we had thoroughly searched the first area.

As we made our way across the grass of the clearing a meadow pipit rose into the air beginning a chirpy trilling song, but he quickly gave it up and fluttered back to the ground some distance off.

"There will be a nest somewhere here, Arthur," I said, "but I think we'll leave the meadow pipit and continue our search for the night jar."

After half an hour of gently parting the bracken and peering down, I eventually found the completely still form of a nightjar. It was elongated on the ground, its chin down, and its eyes almost shut, yet I knew the bird was totally alert and taking in my every move.

"Over here, Arthur," I called very softly, "but come very slowly and quietly."

Arthur gingerly made his way across to stand beside me and we both looked down at the beautiful greys, fawns, browns and charcoal colourings of the softly mottled plumage. We studied the bird for a while before gently backing away and leaving the bird in peace.

"Beautiful, but quite strange," said Arthur when we were clear of the bracken.

"Yes, Arthur, it is an odd mixture of beauty and near ugliness. Its rather stubby and bristly bill is scarcely attractive. When the bird opens its bill to take moths it has an enormous gape. And had you been able to see them it has funny little legs, almost as if deformed. Yet for all that it's a compelling bird."

"Was that its nest," asked Arthur.

"Yes, I rather think it was. She just lays her long oval eggs on the ground. There is no nest, as such, just a little scrape."

As we began to make our way back to the *vardo* where I suspected Raq would be more than ready to be let out to scamper around, I resumed my train of though about birds on the ground.

"Of course, nightjars roost on the ground during the day, Arthur, so had it been a male bird there would be no reason to suppose that there was a nest," I continued.

"How could you tell it was a hen bird, Romany?" asked Arthur.

"By the lack of the white markings on wings, tail and throat," I replied.

From the trees beyond us came a beautiful fluting song, less powerful than a blackbird, but quite enchanting.

Blackcap

"A blackcap," I said in reply to Arthur's inquisitive look.

Raq was delighted to see us when we reached the *vardo*, and he bounded around wildly, coming back every few seconds to lick us both in turn. We had become so engrossed in our search for the nightjar that we had missed our lunch. We therefore decided on an early supper instead, and to that end we got a good *yog* (fire) crackling away, and set up the irons to suspend the pot.

I had plans to keep the fire going through the evening, so while I prepared the rabbit I had picked up the previous evening, Arthur went off in search of more firewood.

After our tasty rabbit stew we sat around the fire well into the night chatting away and recounting the birds and animals we had seen since I had arrived in Cumberland at the end of the previous year. It had been pleasing for me to watch Arthur's interest in the world of Nature blossom and develop.

Somehow we got onto the subject of plants and Gypsy remedies. I had learned of many of these from my Romani mother, but fear that I had forgotten more than I could remember.

"While we were up on the Fells by the broom I remembered that Gypsies use an infusion of broom leaves to relieve kidney complaints," I said, then added, "and thinking of the bracken we've been in today, that's a cure for constipation."

An owl hooted in the distance, and bats flickered overhead, as we sat comfortably by the glow of the fire.

"Saint John's wort is supposed to make the hair grow, but I don't know whether it works," I continued; "And then there's the pennyroyal – that's used for colds and chills."

I thought for a bit and then added, "Burdock is used to relieve rheumatism. Crushed seeds work best. Anyway, Arthur, I think that's enough to give you an idea."

"I am enjoying this life, Romany," said Arthur.

"Yes, I am too, but it can be a hard life at times; however, I've never met a Traveller who doesn't think that the rewards far outweigh the hardships," I said.

We were distracted by a series of grunting and rustling noises. I had heard this so many times before I knew what it was without even turning round.

"That's a *hotchi witchi*," I said.

"A *what?*" replied Arthur.

"A hedgehog. Sorry, as we had been talking about Gypsy things I automatically used its Romani name!" I explained.

The hedgehog must have caught our scent, for after pausing for a while sniffing the air he shuffled off back the way he had come.

"Once, when I was sitting rather like this I heard a lot of clanging coming from under the *vardo*. It turned out to be a hedgehog that had got its head stuck fast in an old tin can which I had inadvertently left on the ground," I told Arthur. "It was a salutary lesson on showing the importance of not leaving things lying around which could be harmful to wildlife."

We talked on for a while discussing farming, for Arthur never seemed to doubt that farming would be his life, the birds and animals to be seen in the area, and also I told Arthur of things I had seen in other areas, especially the birds of the coastal cliffs.

"Bed now, I think, Arthur," I said at last, and making sure the fire was safe, we turned in, Arthur to the *vardo*, and I to my sleeping bag under the waggon – the weather had been too good for me to bother with a tent.

Chapter 16

Home and away

The next day, after breakfast, we cleared up our camp and harnessed Comma for the journey home. Arthur decided to walk with Comma, so Raq, who often sat beside me on the footboard, trotted along with him as well. I had considered taking an alternative route back to Glassonby, but bridges over the Eden are so far and few between it didn't make sense. If we had gone down to the bridge at Langwathby it would have added a day to our journey. We, therefore, passed through Lazonby and crossed, as we had on our way out, at Eden Bridge.

"Arthur," I called as we came off the bridge, "look at the patient angler down there."

Arthur looked, and then said, "I can't see anyone, Romany. Just a heron."

I smiled and told him, "It was the heron I was referring to."

"Sorry," said Arthur chuckling.

We stopped and watched the heron for a while. He was so still it was difficult to believe that he hadn't fallen asleep. All doubt as to that, however, was completely removed when in a fraction of a second he had shot his head down and speared

Heron

a small fish, probably a trout par. He raised his head high to swallow his prize, took two steady paces on his long lanky, legs, and resumed his hunched position to await another unwary fish.

A little further on we pulled off the road to have our lunch. We then continued to Kirkoswald and from there on down to Daleraven Bridge and finally back to Glassonby.

"Can I come straight up to Old Parks and have one more night in the *vardo*, Romany? Please?" asked Arthur as we neared Midtown Farm.

"I think you should just pop home to make sure it's all right with your parents, Arthur. It's certainly all right with me," I replied.

I pulled up so that Arthur could let his family know that we were safely back, and to see if he could spend the night up at Old Parks. A moment later Arthur came bounding back with a grin so wide I knew the answer had been yes! And so we made our way to Glassonby Beck, where Comma deftly manoeuvred the *vardo* round the tight bends at the narrow bridge, and on up to Old Parks where we received a warm welcome from Joe and Sallie.

Once the *vardo* was parked in its old spot I took Comma along to the yard. Joe took her head and led her off to join his own horses.

"Don't get too used to having her back, Joe," I called out.

"Why? Are ye off again soon? More birdwatching?" Joe responded.

"Something like that, Joe," I said, as I turned on my heel and went back to the *vardo*.

The truth was that our little excursion to Lazonby Fell had made me restless. I love the Fells; I love Old Parks; but I now felt that old urge that my ancestors before me knew so well, and I knew that it would not be long before I would 'jal the *drom*' – go on the road again.

Just as I was deciding what to prepare for our supper, Joe appeared with a white cloth covering a huge pie.

"Sallie thought you might like this to save you cooking on your first night back," he said; "It's still warm."

"How every kind," I said, "Do thank her. We shall both enjoy it."

Joe strode off with a cheery wave and Arthur and I made short work of Sallie's meat and vegetable pie. It was delicious and the gravy sauce in the pie was especially tasty.

"How about an evening stroll before we turn in?" I suggested.

"I'm ready," said Arthur jumping up.

We headed up the track towards High Barn. It was a lovely moonlit evening again and we saw no reason to take a lamp. Raq, having trotted a good deal of the way back from Lazonby Fell was quite content to walk sedately beside us rather than run ahead, run back, and run ahead again as he often did.

As the outline of the High Barn loomed on the horizon ahead of us, a sound floated down to us – a drawn out "squeee."

"Barn owl," I said. "If we keep still we may see it flying."

Obligingly the owl appeared from High Barn and flew in our direction. We kept completely still. It passed quite close to us before veering off to avoid us.

"Did you hear its wings when it got close, Arthur?" I asked.

"I'm afraid I didn't," he replied rather apologetically.

"Exactly," I said. "Owls make no sound when they fly because the wing feathers are especially soft so that they make no sound. That allows them to hunt their prey down

Barn owl

111

without giving any warning of their approach."

From the brow of the hill at High Barn we looked out towards the Lake District. Being such a clear night we could see the lights of Penrith and several villages beyond. After taking in the scene for a while we turned back down the hill and returned to the *vardo*.

"Thank you, Romany," said Arthur as he climbed up into the *vardo*. "I have really enjoyed myself these past few days."

"It's been a pleasure to have your company, Arthur," I replied.

I left him to assemble the bed – he was quite expert at it now – and I retired to my tent. I had left it up while we were away.

The next morning, before Arthur went home, I suggested that we go down to the beck and dismantle our hide as the dippers had now left the nest. Despite this, we approached cautiously and crawled into the hide to see if anything was about before we started to take it down. As we peeped out there was a flash of electric blue and a kingfisher alighted on the dippers' favourite rock. It had its vivid blue back towards us, but the breeze was blowing towards it, fluffing out its orangey chestnut flank feathers.

Kingfisher

"Wow," said Arthur softly; "I've seen a distant streak of blue along the beck a few times, but I've never had a close up view like that before."

"It has been a nice final bonus from the dipper hide," I said. Once the kingfisher flew off we took down the hide and laid the branches in a pile at the edge of the trees. If Joe wanted to collect some of it for firewood it was now easily accessible. If he didn't then it would make a good home for a variety of wild creatures.

Over the next few days my mind kept returning to the idea of taking to the road again. I knew that Arthur would be disappointed so I decided on one last expedition before I left, but what should it be? Arthur's father provided the answer. He told me that he needed to go to Hexham, and that he would be quite happy to drop me off on the Fells and then pick me up again on his way home.

"That's a wonderful idea, John," I said. "And can your Arthur come with me?"

"Of course he can," he replied, "if you're sure he'll not be any hindrance."

"Certainly not," I assured him; "It is wonderful to find a lad so interested in and concerned for the natural world around him."

John Kidd smiled proudly at my reply.

Although Arthur didn't yet know it, this was my last adventure with him, so when we waved goodbye to Arthur's father as he drove away after dropping us off on the roadside a few days later, and we began to walk out onto the Fells, I was really hoping that we would find something memorable. There were plenty of meadow pipits – a good larder for the merlins, as Arthur put it – and, music to my ears, curlews!

"Go-back, go-back, go-back," came the nasal call of a red grouse.

"I reckon he knows he's safe from guns this time of year," commented Arthur with a grin, as the bird allowed us to get fairly close before speeding off on whirring wings, low over the heather.

"You could be right," I said, then added urgently, "Quick, Arthur, look over

Red grouse

there."

It was a merlin dashing over the moor ahead of us. Although we were on a different part of the Fells from where we had watched the merlin before, I though we were probably still within its territory, in which case, we were some way off from where we knew it to be nesting.

"No point in waiting for him to return," I said; "He was hunting this area but may not come back for hours or even days, depending on how well he does for food nearer home."

"Look, Romany," said Arthur. "That's the third of these little red butterflies I've seen."

I followed the direction of his pointing hand, and said, "Let's see if we can get a little closer now it's settled."

Cinnabar moth

We carefully edged forward and looked down on the lovely red and charcoal grey wings of the creature.

"Still think it's a butterfly, Arthur?" I asked. "Well, it's broad daylight so it can't be a moth," he answered, but with a little hesitation. He then added, "but I think I remember from nature lessons at school that butterflies sit with their wings closed together upwards, but moths have them flat...... like this."

"Well done, Arthur," I commended him, "that's exactly right. This is a cinnabar moth, and they are really quite happy to be out in the daylight. We might think of him as the exception that proves the rule!"

We continued our walk for a while and then sat down to a hearty lunch, provided once again by Arthur's mother. As we sat there we heard a rapid "kee, kee, kee" above us. Looking up we could see the unmistakable outline of a peregrine falcon. It looked rather like an overgrown swift.

"Next time I come to Glassonby, we'll see if we can find a nesting peregrine to watch," I said, as an opening to broach the subject of my departure.

"Why *next* time," asked the lad, as I rather thought he would.

"Because, Arthur, I shall be moving off soon," I explained. Arthur looked taken aback then crestfallen.

"So soon," he pleaded.

Peregrine falcon

"Soon?" I exclaimed, "I've been here since the back end of last autumn."

"Yes, I suppose you have," Arthur conceded, "but I shall miss our walks."

"I shall too, Arthur," I told him,"but you can still go out looking for wildlife yourself. And I will be back one day. Old Parks is under my skin, as they say."

We walked on in silence for a while, then as we were reaching one of those myriad horizons one sees ahead when Fell walking, only to find when you get there that there is another hill beyond, I dropped to the ground and gestured to Arthur to do the same. On the next brow there was a handsome black and gold bird. I handed Arthur my binoculars.

"It's a golden plover," I said; "Same family as the lapwing."

"He is *beautiful,*" said Arthur appreciatively.

"Indeed he is," I agreed.

"Do they nest up here," asked the boy.

"They do," I replied, "but like all plovers they just lay their eggs on the ground. I daresay his mate is sitting somewhere up there."

"Can we go and find her?" asked Arthur.

"I think not. If we don't start to make our way off the Fell and back down to the road we won't be back by the time we agreed with your father," I pointed out.

Golden plover

After one final look at the beautifully marked plover we began to wend our way back. Not for the first time I was appreciative of Arthur's intuitive silence as we drank in the sights, sounds and smells of the moorland we were leaving. It had been a really good day. I just hoped that it was not too marred for Arthur knowing that I was leaving.

That evening I broke my news to Joe and Sallie. They were not surprised. They knew my ways and had half suspected that my journey to Lazonby Fell had been but a prelude to wider wanderings.

The following day I packed up my belongings, dismantled my tent and my temporary dark room, checked Comma over and then backed her into the shafts of the *vardo*. I had said farewell to Arthur and his family the previous evening so now I just had to say my goodbyes to Joe, Sallie, and young Desmond. They all stood in the farmyard and waved as I negotiated the *vardo* out through the yard gate onto the track down to the Glassonby road. Of course, I felt some sadness, but I knew I could return – I always did. Now, however, there were pastures new ahead. I flicked the reins and we rumbled down the track, I knew not where. A plan would form itself. It always did.

Glossary of *Romani* (Gypsy) words used

atch, atched	Stop, stopped; stay, staying
av	come
akai, acoi	here
chitty	tripod of irons for the fire
drom	road, way
hotchi witchi	hedgehog
jal	go
juke, jukal	dog
kushti, kushto	good
vardo	caravan, cart
yog	fire

The Author

Phil Shelley was born in Liverpool in the early 1950's. He developed an interest in wildlife after moving North of the city in his formative years. Birdwatching remains a passion, although he is also an avid guitarist and singer, making recordings in his studio.

He is a director of a Coventry-based business, where he is located during the week, commuting home at weekends.

Romany's life, works and environmental ideals have become something of an obsession with Phil. He wouldn't say so himself, but he is almost certainly the UK's most knowledgeable person with regard to Romany.

The Artist and co-author

R Leonard Hollands obOSB MRICS MFPWS MASI MRSPH, was born in 1942 and studied art initially at the Heston and Isleworth Evening Institute whilst also an architectural trainee, and then, on a one to one basis, under Bertram Armitage, son of Alfred Armitage, minor artist of the Newlyn School.

He is first and foremost a Wildlife Artist, his special interest, as a life-long ornithologist, being bird paintings in which he endeavours to create an "alive" image (some of them have been used as cards for the RSPB of which he is a Life Fellow), but, taking his inspiration from the marvels of Creation, he also paints abstracts and landscapes. His work, therefore, is varied and of wide appeal. He works mainly in oil and acrylic and sometimes in gouache.

More of his work can be seen at
www.rleonardhollands.co.uk

Other books by Phil Shelley

Romany in the Lanes

Other books by R Leonard Hollands

Susan's Adventures
Mystery at the Hermitage
Mystery of Pipers' Keil
Katrine – Contrasts and Eclipses
My Sea Eagle Odyssey
The Wildlife Drawings of Brendon Hollands
An Orthodox Prayer Book

Other Romany Books

A Romany in the Fields	By Romany
A Romany and Raq	"
A Romany in the Country	"
A Romany on the Trail	"
Out with Romany	"
Out with Romany Again	"
Out with Romany Once More	"
Out with Romany by the Sea	"
Out with Romany by Meadow and Stream	"
Out with Romany by Moor and Dale	"
Through the Years with Romany	Eunice Evens
Romany Turns Detective	G K Evens
Romany, Muriel and Doris	"
Romany on the Farm	"
Romany's Caravan Returns	"

These books have long been out of print, but the **Romany Society** has a book service and can provide most of these titles second hand. In recent years some of these books been re-issued by Isis in large print, and some as audio books.

Details of all this can be found on the Romany Society website: **www.romanysociety.org.uk**

www.ingramcontent.com/pod-product-compliance
Lightning Source LLC
Chambersburg PA
CBHW052206170626
46812CB00004B/1669